Saving Sun and Moon:

The Quest of the Almost-Goddess

Sorcha Monk

First edition 2023

Cover artist: getcovers.com

epub ISBN: 978-1-961616-00-4

hardcover ISBN: 978-1-961616-01-1

paperback ISBN: 978-1-961616-02-8

Spot Ox Publishing

To everyone who ever told me a story...

Thank you.

Contents

Chapter One: The Girl

N eddy counted on her fingers for added emphasis, trying to impress her teacher with how smart she was.

"On my Quest, I leave the Galenwood," she folded over her first finger and took a moment to look around her at those very woods. "Find my hero. Grab a handful of dust," she continued and folded two more fingers. "Bring the dust back, and do it all before Sun and Moon face each other across the world and the stars make a bridge between them." The last two fingers and thumb folded, and she held up a triumphant, if not very clean, fist. An unruly red curl fell in her face. She tried to coax the defiant hair behind one ear, but it jumped right back out again.

"Yes," said Rebane, her teacher. "But that wasn't what we were talking about." Rebane had the patience of stone because he was a golem made of obsidian. He'd been Neddy's teacher since her first day, which had been a very, very long time ago. "Now, remember why we're here. What are you supposed to be doing?" he said, looking around the clearing where they stood.

"Runestones. I'm collecting runestones." Neddy focused her attention back to searching the ground and, seeing a pebble that might make a good one, she bent to pick it up. A pocket appeared in the skirt of her clean, white frock – it was always clean, free of dirt and grass stains, unlike the girl who wore it – and she slipped the stone in. The pocket disappeared.

CRASH!

A huge deer charged out of the trees, jumping over the low shrubs edging the clearing. Nostrils flared and eyes wide in fear, it raced directly towards them.

"Hunter!" The stag shrieked as it ran.

Neddy ducked, throwing her arms over her head and flattening herself to the ground. The hooves soared over her, digging holes in the ground when the animal stopped. It turned to look from where it had leapt, hot breath steaming from its heaving lungs.

Rising to her feet, Neddy wiped the grass from her knees and elbows. She flicked a wild strand of hair from her mouth, and stood to face the stag.

"What kind of hunter?"

"A hairy two-legger!" The deer's feet shuffled backwards to gain traction. It lowered its head and growled. "A human."

Neddy looked to her teacher. "A human? There shouldn't be any humans here. Only the people of the forest are allowed in these woods."

"And what do you think should be done about this?" Rebane tilted his head.

Neddy turned toward the trees. She pulled at the small white twig that was stuck in her tangled mane, vainly attempting to keep the wild curls in order. She whispered a few words and dropped the twig onto the grass where it bounced a few times then turned into a huge, white tree. The stag stepped behind it.

~~~~~~

Heavy leather boots stomped through the trees, not caring whether they landed on dirt or grass or the flower that had only today woken up to see the sky. The man was large, both in height and width. His face was crimson with exertion, and hairy, red-splotched arms protruded from the rolled-up sleeves of a grungy tunic. A bulky fist full of gnarled knuckles grasped a long wooden bow and a quiver full of heavy arrows was slung across his back. As he reached the clearing the hunter's eyes scanned the area for the magnificent antlers he'd followed through the woods. He thought of how handsome they were going to look, still attached to the beast's head, mounted on a piece of wood, and hung over the mantlepiece above his fireplace. *There.* There they were… behind the tree. The pointed tines blended with the white branches. But not well enough.

"Now, if you'll just hold still….," the hunter breathed. He lifted the bow and reached back for an arrow.

From the corner of an eye the hunter saw the young girl watching him from a few feet away. She wore a simple white dress and no shoes. She was about the size of most children he knew, which weren't many, and a feral mass of red hair the color of ripe berries fell down her back. She held her hands together in front of her and the tune she was quietly humming to herself was unfamiliar to him.

The hunter tried to focus on his prey, tried to ignore the distraction. Tried not to wonder what a young girl not more than twelve years old was doing, all by herself, out here in the woods.

She looked no more than twelve years old to him. But if he had been paying attention to where he was he would have known she was much, much older than that.

The humming grew a little louder.

The hunter lowered his bow for a moment to wipe the sweat from his face with a sleeve. "Hush, girl!" he hissed. He notched the arrow against the string again and closed one eye, using the other to focus on where the heart would be when the animal stepped out from its hiding place.

"You're not supposed to be here," the girl said in a sing-song voice, barely loud enough for the man to hear.

The hunter ignored her.

Hands on her hips, the girl pulled herself to her full height – almost tall enough for the top of her head to reach his elbow. A bracelet, braided strands of silver with a pendant with a moon on one side and a sun on the other, slid down her small wrist. "What are you doing here?"

"Girl!" he growled. "Can't you see? …I've … almost… got him…."

"Him?" Neddy looked to where the man was aiming. "Who is him?"

"The stag. Behind that tree." The bowstring was taut.

Neddy stood on her tiptoes, her hand over her eyes as if blocking the sun. "I don't see anything. Are you sure he's there?"

"Yes! Now hush."

"It's not nice to *hush* somebody," Neddy said. "Besides, you're not supposed to be here. You should leave."

"Can you please be quiet? You'll scare him off."

"Oh! I think I see him now. You can almost just see the antlers just in the middle of those branches." She said the last part a bit louder than the other parts. The antlers moved and disappeared behind the trunk of the tree.

The man grunted, let the air from his lungs, and re-positioned his weapon.

It was quiet for a few moments. The man frozen in place with his bow and arrow focused on the animal behind the tree.

"You know," Neddy said, making the man wince, "you really aren't supposed to be here. You should leave before you're sorry."

"As soon as I get those antlers you'll never see me again…."

"Do you know where you are?"

Large shoulders dropped slightly, his eyes glancing aside at the girl, "In the woods," he hissed. He went back to focusing on the stag. "What are you? Lost or something?"

"*I* know where we are," she stated matter of factly. "But, do *you* know where we are?"

"We're in a place where I could get this stag if only you would be quiet!"

Crossing her arms in front of her thin chest, Neddy stared at the man.

"We're in the woods," the man grumbled. "Now, hush!"

The piercing gaze was unnerving.

"What?" The hunter lowered his bow, resigning himself to the fact that he might not be claiming a magnificent set of antlers today. "What is it that you want?"

"You're right," the girl narrowed her eyes. "We are in the woods."

"And? What of it?"

"Which woods?"

"I dunno. It's just a woods. A forest like any other."

"It has a name," the girl said. "You're in the Galenwood."

"Hahah!" he laughed, then stopped. "Wait. You're serious."

"Yes."

"Galenwood. That's a myth," he turned to the girl, his voice more condescending than kind. "Old women tell children... little girls like yourself, no offence... they tell the children stories of the *Galenwood*," he loosely waved his hands around and up, wiggling his thick fingers, *"magic forest, enchanted trees, witches.…* They tell it to scare the young ones and keep them from running out and getting lost."

"There *is* some magic here, but the trees aren't enchanted. They're just very much alive. No witches either," she shook her head. "This is the Galenwood."

"Galenwood."

"Yes."

As sure as he was a minute ago, the man started feeling a bit unsure and thought maybe he should be going home. He took a step backward, bumping into a tree that hadn't been there before. He felt behind him and tried to move his body around the knotted trunk. It moved with him. Something worse than fear spun in the innermost workings of his bowels when thick branches reached around his chest, holding him in place.

From behind him, the tree's limbs reached out and pulled the bow from his hand and the arrows from the quiver, dropping them on the ground where he watched them decompose and melt into the soil.

Tears of dread leaked from the corners of the hunter's eyes as the girl – just a little girl! – leaned close to him. Her eyes were the color of the morning sky. "You can come out now," she said.

If the man hadn't known where he was before, *he knew now* as he watched the tree shrink to a twig. The stag grasped the white stick in its teeth and brought it to Neddy, and she wove it back into the twists of her hair. She reached up and rested an arm across the deer's back.

"I didn't know!" the hunter pleaded.

"Didn't you?"

"I am safe here," the deer growled. "You cannot hunt me within these woods."

Neddy understood the deer's words. The man, however, did not speak the universal language, and all he heard was gruff, snorting sounds.

"He doesn't understand," Neddy said to the stag.

"I can *make* him understand," the deer lowered his head, menacing the man with the many points of his antlers.

"No," said Neddy, "I think maybe we could give him a chance." She called to the golem. "Rebane, do you think this could be a chance for me to get some practice?"

Rebane nodded and stood back, folding his massive arms.

Neddy smiled and turned to the man, and spoke in the language he would understand. "When I give the word, this tree will let you go. When it does, you run. Run as fast as you can. Leave the Galenwood."

9

"Oh, thank you!" the man cried, already looking for which way he would run once loose. "Thank you for having mercy on me."

"Mercy? Maybe. Maybe not," Neddy said. "You *will* run as fast as you can, away from here."

The hunter nodded, "Yes! Of course!" His eyes darted towards the trees behind him, thinking more of his escape than what the girl was saying.

"I am going to take this moment to practice my spelling. You will run and if you reach the edge of the Galenwood before my spell catches you, you are free. Go home. Never return."

"Yes! Of course! I'll run away! You'll never see me in this place again!"

"But if the spell catches you," Neddy continued, "you will be whatever I have spelled you to be."

"What?" the man yelped. His thick arms strained against the wooden restraints, his feet kicked at the ground, vainly trying to get away.

Neddy nodded to the tree, and the man was released.

"Run," she said to the hunter. "Now."

Eyes wide, hands sweating, he stumbled the first few steps but soon was running as fast as he'd ever run in his life. *For* his life. He wanted to look over his shoulder, to see what the girl was doing, but didn't dare. Look forward. Run through a path that disappeared as fast as it appeared. Jump over roots that seemed to rise above the ground, somehow knowing exactly where the next foot would land. Dodge the bushes that leapt in in front of him. He was sure he'd lost his way, then sure he'd found it. In the distance, through the trees, he saw the grassy field that bordered the Galenwood. Leaning forward he gathered everything in his gut to get away.

Neddy reached for the skirt of her dress. A pocket appeared. She retrieved a piece of twine and a white pebble from it. The pocket disappeared back into the folds. She rolled the stone and string between the palms of her hands, whispering to them as they grew warm and the twine wrapped itself around the pebble. She whispered some more, then tossed the ball into the air. Another word, a flick of her wrist, and a breeze carried the ball of string and stone away – in the direction in which the man had run.

Chapter Two: The Woman

E rda walked through the woods in the chilled dark that covers the world just before daybreak. The black cloak draped around her shoulders never caught a branch, her red tunic and trousers never snagged a bramble, and the trees and shrubbery gently shifted to clear the way for her. Creatures that lived in the forest quietly watched her go by. Erda was a Galenor, the Goddess of the Galenwood, where she lived.

Alongside Erda walked Neddy. Her dress as white as the first day she wore it, which was about the only thing about her that was tidy. Defiant red hair escaped from the white twig trying to hold it in place. Her knees and elbows were stained the color of grass.

"Rebane tells me you met a hunter during your lessons," said Erda.

"He wasn't supposed to be here," Neddy explained. "I tried to warn him."

Erda had seen humans in the Galenwood but, while it was true that they weren't permitted here, there were other ways to deal with them. "Could you have given him a choice?"

"Rebane said it was okay."

"That's not what I asked."

Neddy thought for a moment. "I did let him run, but I didn't give him a choice."

"Do you think you should have?"

Neddy thought for another moment. "Not really," she answered. "I don't think he would have blended in well here. He wasn't a good human."

"Hmm… You might be right. In the Galenwood the wayward human should be given a choice, but some don't deserve it."

As they strolled across the glen, Erda looked up and wondered if she should be concerned. The sun was well into the clear sky, but the shadows weren't right for this time of day. They were gray like you'd expect beneath hazy clouds, even though today the sky was clear. She sensed something was wrong but couldn't tell what it was.

"Here it is," said Erda, kneeling in front of the raccoon's den where three kits had been born the night before. A pocket appeared in the drape of her tunic. She pulled a small stone from it, and the pocket disappeared. "Watch closely," she said to Neddy and, holding the smooth rock between her palms, she whispered and gently blew into the clasped hands. The stone pulsed with a warm glow like the moon and sun combined. Colors swirled, etching a sigil into the stone. Erda whispered to it one more time then buried it at the entrance to the den.

Erda's skin prickled. "Did you feel that?" she asked Neddy.

"I did."

"Good. It's important to always pay attention to the world around you. Now, let's go see what caused it."

~~~~~~

The boy made his way through the trees and bushes. He knew he shouldn't be here, but it was better than anywhere else he could be. Even with trees that grabbed at him, roots that rose to trip him, and bushes that made pathways disappear it was still better than where he'd come from. He watched the ground as he walked, hopping over vines and rocks that rolled in front of his feet. He stopped when he saw the statue.

It was of a man. A running man. The eyes were wide, and fear covered not just the face, but somehow the entire body. The boy recognized the heavy boots. They'd often kicked at him when he was looking for something to eat in the alley behind the butcher's shop. The boy also recognized the man. The village butcher.

"Your wife is nice," the boy said to the man of stone. "She gives me food when you're away." It occurred to the boy that the butcher had been gone for several days longer than usual. *Odd*, he thought. *But, even odder… why is there a statue of you out here in the woods?* He swung back a leg to give the man a good kick but, remembering it was a man made of rock, thought better of it. He reached down into the moist soil, made a mudball and threw it with all his might, hitting the butcher squarely on the face. The boy added to his sense of satisfaction with a hand gesture and a few of the words the man had often yelled at him. Not nice words. Not words he would say to his mother if he had one. Not words the butcher's wife ever said, that was certain.

And then the ground left his feet.

Flying from tree to tree, the boy was tossed over, in and around the canopy. Branches caught, swung and tossed him again and again. Fear or delight? The boy wasn't sure what he felt, but he laughed at every airborne moment and held his breath at every catch. Through the woods he went. Lobbed, thrown, chucked, and hurled until one final fling sent him higher into the air than he'd ever been.

Well, he thought, *that was fun, but I guess this is it for me.* He closed his eyes and wondered if he would hear the thud when he fell to his death.

But he didn't fall to his death.

~~~~~~

Erda and Neddy ran. Erda's thick black hair cascaded in waves behind her, with wind under her feet. A necklace, braided strands of silver, held close to her neck, the pendant with a sun on one side and a moon on the other, bounced gently against her skin. Alongside her, Neddy hurried to keep up.

They reached the clearing, stopped, and watched the boy flying from tree to tree. A smile came to Erda's lips when she heard the boy's laughter. It was a certain kind of laughter that she didn't hear very often. Especially not from someone being thrown between branches.

With a final lob the boy flew high into the air. Erda reached for the long, black feather that was tucked snugly into her thick hair. She tossed it in the air where it hovered for a moment, then rose, floating upwards. When it reached a height above the trees, it burst into a storm of feathers, each transforming into an incredibly large raven. They flew to the falling boy and surrounded him, beating their wings to slow the fall until they reached the ground. Gently, they set him on the grass and, forming a half-circle around the boy, they nodded to Erda and stood back.

Neddy watched as Erda approached the boy. Colors of fear softly rippled from him. This was odd. The fear was there, but it wasn't much more than a tinge compared to the overpowering colors of wonder. And of innocence. Kneeling close enough to feel the boy's breath, Erda looked into his widened eyes.

"We don't see ones like you very often," Erda said. She looked up, nodding to the birds. The air whooshed with flapping wings as they found perches in the trees where they could watch. Squirrels watched, too. And rabbits. Bees, bugs, insects. Everything in the clearing, even the trees, watched. They wanted to see what Erda would do.

"You're where you're not supposed to be," the woman said to the boy. "How old are you?"

"I don't know," the boy said. Something in the back of his mind told him he should be afraid. But something even further back, stronger, told him there was nothing to fear. He decided to listen to the stronger voice.

"You don't know?"

"No," the boy said. "I've no one to tell me when I was born. But I'm as big as those other boys who go to school every day."

"You have no family?"

The sad silence was enough of an answer.

"Do you know where you are?" the woman asked.

The boy looked around. "Well....," he considered thoughtfully, "I was in the woods and now I'm in a field. He looked at the woman a little bit sideways. "Why are there statues in the woods?"

"Those are people who came where they're not supposed to be."

"I recognized one," the boy said. "The butcher. He's mean." The boy's eyes widened. "Are you saying that's not just a statue? It's really him?"

Erda nodded.

"I.... I...," the boy stammered, knowing it was wrong to think what he was thinking. To feel the little bit of joy he felt. Then he blurted, "He always kicked me when I would come around. All I asked for was a few scraps. He was throwing them out anyway. His wife is nice, though. Whenever he's gone she gives me somethin' to eat." He paused, seeing the pieces of a puzzle come together. "Nobody's seen him in a while. I guess now I know why."

Erda sat down, stretching her legs out in front of her and, putting her hands on the grass behind her, she leaned back on her arms and looked across the field. She patted the ground at her side, beckoning the boy to sit next to her.

"Do you have a name?" she asked.

"There's things people call me," the boy said, "but not an official... not a real name." He looked at the woman. "Do you have a name?" He might not have had an upbringing, but he knew what manners were. It was polite to contribute to the conversation. And, besides, he did want to know who she was.

"I am Erda," she answered. She gestured behind her, "This is Neddy. We are the Galenorae."

The boy didn't know how to respond to this, so he said, "oh." He sat next to the woman, stretching out his legs and leaning back on his arms, just like her. "Pleased to meet you."

On Erda's nod, Neddy joined them and they sat in silence for a while.

After a while, the boy asked, "What's a Gladdenory?"

Erda smiled. "Galenorae. We watch over and care for the Galenwood," said Erda.

The boy nodded, but said nothing.

"Do you know what the Galenwood is?" Erda asked

"No," he answered. "Is that what this place is?"

"Yes." Erda said. "Humans are forbidden from entering here. And once they enter they're not allowed to leave."

"I can't ever leave?"

"No."

The boy didn't feel too bad about it, but then he thought about the butcher.

"Is that why the butcher's a statue? Did you do that?"

"I did," said Neddy.

"I'd rather not be turned to stone," he said.

Erda smiled. "Not everyone gets turned to stone," she gave a quick look to Neddy, but spoke to the boy. "Sometimes someone like you comes along. Someone without bad intentions. Someone with a true heart." She paused, letting a squirrel jump onto her lap. "You have a pure heart, like the people of the Galenwood."

"People? I haven't seen any people."

"No, not human-people. In the Galenwood, the *people* are the ones that live here. Like this little squirrel. The deer. The raccoons. Bugs, birds…. Everything. They are the people of the Galenwood." The squirrel hopped from her lap to the boy's, playfully brushing his nose with its bushy tail. "People like you get to choose."

"Choose?"

"What would you like to be?"

The boy hesitated. "I'm not sure I understand what you mean."

"If you could be any animal, any animal in the world, what would you be?"

The boy considered this for a bit then asked, "Do you have a pond here?"

"The Galenwood has everything. It has woods for the deer, fields for the mice, trees for the birds, lakes and ponds for the fish…"

"A pond would be fine," the boy grinned. "I'd like to be a frog."

"A frog?"

"Yes," he nodded. "To be able to hop. And to be able to live in the water *and* on land. Croaking and catching flies with my tongue!" He emphasized the last point by flicking his own tongue quickly in and out of his mouth.

Erda stood, stretching out her arms. The ravens flew down from the trees, floating on air in a spiral above around her head. Saying words the boy had never heard before, she clapped her hands. Feathers burst into the air, weaving themselves together, dropping into the woman's hand as the one feather they had been before. Erda tucked the feather into her hair, and reached out a hand to the boy.

"Let's walk," she said, "I'll show you where the pond is."

The three made their way from the field to a line of gently sloping hills, leading the boy over the knoll, and stopping at the top so they could both take a moment to look the Galenwood.

Behind them, across the field, was the forest from where the boy had come, and in front of them the hills sloped downward into brambles and brush. In the distance the boy could see the river that he knew passed the village where he'd been living until now. He turned in a circle, taking it in, stopping when he saw the massive stone in the middle of it all. It rose higher than the trees. Even from this distance he could see it rippled with an iridescent sheen, with steps carved into it, spiraling around to the top that was flat and wide.

"What's that?" he asked.

"We call it the Galen Tower. It's where we meet when we need to."

"You can see everything from up here, can't you?"

"Almost," said Erda, She waited a moment, then said, "Are you ready?"

"Yes, I think I am." The boy smiled up at the woman, then looked at Neddy and remembered the hunter. "No offense," he said to the girl, "but I'd feel more comfortable if it was the lady who was doing the magic."

"That's okay," said Neddy. "I might not trust me either."

"Okay then," said the boy. He looked at Erda. "Let's go."

They walked across the low hills and through a valley full of flowers and grass, until they reached the muddy edge of a lily-covered pond. Frogs – so many of them… big, small, dark green, light green, speckled, spotted – greeted them with croaks and splashes.

Erda reached into a pocket that appeared in her tunic and disappeared after she pulled out a pinch of dust. A drop of spit and the dust was clay that she molded into a skull. A frog's skull. She scooped up a handful of pond scum. And she molded it all into a ball. She whispered something into the clasped hands, smiled at the boy and, holding the ball in a fist over her head, said, "Enjoy living the rest of your days as a frog." And she threw it at him.

~~~~~~

It was a strange sensation, turning into a frog. Bones clicked. Skin turned green. Innards changed size and place inside him. The brain reshaped itself to forget being human and to think of frog things. And everything shrunk. It didn't happen fast. But it didn't take a long time, either.

Low to the ground, the frog who had been a little boy tested his new self, lifting one toe, a back leg, giving himself a little hop. He turned to Erda, blinked his round eyes, and happily croaked, "This is the best day of my life!" He was surprised when words came out of his mouth.

"It's the universal language," Erda told him. "Everyone – everything – in the Galenwood speaks it. Outside, only those who remember it do."

The newly-frogged boy flicked his tongue at a fly, and missed. But it didn't matter. He hopped to the edge of the water, swam across the pond, and climbed onto a lily pad. His tongue flicked in and out, and he laughed with the other frogs who sat on lily pads around him.

Erda smiled, then looked up at the sky, towards the sun. And she wondered....

Neddy looked to the sky, too, and wondered what it was that Erda was sensing.

Chapter Three: The Crone

Gerte, the Crone of the Galenorae, set some water to boil and went to the rack holding assorted containers above the hearth. Running her old fingers across the jars, she selected the one filled with the dried petals of four-leafed clovers. Letting the clover tea steep, she sat in front of the fire that slowly burned against the wall.

She held the earthen mug with both hands, as she slowly sipped the tea. The chair, as ancient as everything else in the cave, rocked silently back and forth. Beneath the curved legs of the rocker was a rug woven of something known only to her, and under the rug was a dirt floor. Streaks of black smudged the stone above the small fire. She didn't really need the fire, as she was never cold, but she liked to watch the dancing flames.

Gerte remembered when Erda had been the Girl, and when she herself had been the Girl. She didn't let herself think about being the Girl again.

Taking one last drink, she drained the liquid from the mug. Eyes closed, hunched forward, holding the cup tightly, she mumbled a few words and peered into it with eyes the color of fog, and she read the remnants of soaked leaves at the bottom. She nodded and clicked her tongue against the backs of her teeth, and tossed the mug into the fire. The Crone stood, pulling the black cowling over her shoulders and the wrinkled black dress, fastening it at her neck with green stick. She let the hood fall and her white hair, pulled back in a thick braid, hung down her back.

Going to the front of her cave, she looked up to the sky. Her black dress rippled above her bare feet like smoke in a breeze, her arms hidden in the long black sleeves. Her eyes were too much into the dusk of age to see for herself, but the leaves had told her. She reached out an arm and called, "Arawn."

A large bird, a lammergeier, flew down from atop the rock above her cave and landed on her wrist. It nibbled at the ring on the woman's thumb. It was silver with suns and moons carved around it.

Gerte stroked the shimmering black feathers of the bird's head. "I need your help, old friend," she said. "Find the Goddess. Find Rebane and the Girl. Tell them we meet at the Galen Tower at sunrise."

Chapter Four: The Quest

"D o you know what this is about?" Neddy asked. A kaleidoscope of butterflies stormed in her stomach.

"Not any more than I did the last time you asked five minutes ago," Rebane answered. Though he was made of stone, his voice was gentle and flowed like dark molasses.

They reached the first moss-covered step in a series that wrapped around the Galen Tower. Made of a single piece of granite, the tower was flat on top with three seats carved into it, facing each other. Erda and Gerte were sitting in two of the seats, waiting.

"Sunrise," the old woman said, gesturing toward the horizon washed in the golden light of a sun already risen. Her smokey tunic moved with her like a thin, black cloud.

"I tried," Neddy said.

Rebane rolled his black eyes.

"My legs are short. I can't walk as fast," Neddy said.

"Never mind," Erda said. "We're all here now."

The old woman turned to Rebane. "Do you think she's ready?"

"She knows her spells," Rebane answered. "She knows runes and sigils. What to whisper, what to keep inside. She knows most of the history. That is," he looked at Neddy, "she knows the parts she listened to."

"I listened," Neddy protested.

"But, as for ready…" Rebane turned back to the old woman, "I don't think that is for me to say."

"The stars are still fairly far away." said Erda, a trace of hope in her voice, but not much. "Maybe there's time for a few more lessons before the Ascension."

"The stars are marching," said Gerte. "They may still be some distance away, but her Quest is going to take longer than the others before her. If she doesn't leave now, the stars will likely arrive to nothing. *You* sensed it. You *know* something is wrong."

"Are you talking about my Quest?" asked Neddy.

Erda and Gerte looked at Neddy, then at each other. Gerte held out a wrinkled hand, palm upwards. The smoky tendrils of her dress rose and covered her hand, then retreated, leaving a small wooden box on the Crone's hand. It was as dark as a starless night. Two strands of string – one golden, the other pale white – tied around it with a knot. "When you're on the bridge of stars, grab a handful of dust from the sky and put it in here." She gave the box to Neddy.

"But it's not time for me to leave yet," Neddy said, staring at the wooden box. It somehow made her feel very small. "The Ascension isn't for a while. There's still time for Moon to dance across the sky with a full belly before I have to go."

"You're right, it *is* early," Gerte said. "But that's not the only way your Quest will be different."

"I won't be leaving the Galenwood?"

"Oh, you'll leave the Galenwood," Erda said.

"You'll also be saving the world," said Gerte.

"What?" Neddy didn't remember Rebane ever telling her of a Quest that saved the world.

"Sun is growing weak," said Erda, pointing to the sunrise that was not quite as brilliant as all the mornings before.

"Dark is returning," said Gerte. "The clover leaves have shown me. Dark has taken the heart from Sun and the breath from Moon."

"We believe Dark sent the Gloks to steal them," Erda added.

Neddy wrinkled her nose at the thought of the Gloks and their stench. Then her eyes grew wide. "Without their heart and breath, Sun has no strength and Moon can't grow full and dance in the sky."

Erda stood and faced the weakened sun. "The Ascension will be here soon, and Gerte is right. The stars are already marching to form the bridge."

"You remember your lessons?" Rebane spoke gently. "The stars must form their bridge between Sun and Moon when they face each other across the horizons. The bridge is what combines the forces of Sun and Moon, and provides the power needed for the Ascension to take place. If Sun and Moon are too weak –"

"If Sun and Moon are too weak, there can be no bridge," Neddy finished her teacher's sentence.

"And there can be no Ascension," said Erda.

"And without the Ascension," said Gerte, "we will no longer… be."

"The world will end," Erda turned to face Neddy. "We will end, all life will end."

"Well," said the old woman, "*We* might end, and all life might end, but the world will not."

"The world will be ruled by Dark," Erda said, "which is nearly the same thing."

"What am *I* supposed to do about that?" Neddy objected. "Dark? Sun? Moon? They're big. I'm just a girl."

"No," said the Crone. "You are *the* Girl."

Erda went back to her seat. "There is someone who can help you."

"In the desert," said Gerte, "there is an old man who dances under a tree in the light of the moon when its belly is full. He is as old as the soil. We are the caretakers of the Galenwood, but he knows the world *outside* the Galenwood better than we can ever hope to. You must find him. He will help you."

"And you must leave now," said Erda. "We don't know how long Moon and Sun can survive without their breath and heart."

~~~~~~~

After the meeting, Rebane and Neddy walked through the night until they reached a cliff at the edge of the Galenwood. At the bottom of the cliff was the river.

Neddy looked over the edge. *This is where all Quests begin,* she thought. *Mine might be different, but it will begin the same as all the others.* She stepped back and looked up at her teacher.

"But *I* haven't noticed anything wrong," Neddy said.

"Your eyes are not like Erda's," Rebane answered. "And the leaves have spoken to the Crone."

"I need to find the old man who dances under the tree –" Neddy said.

"Yes."

"— when Moon's belly is full."

"So we are told."

"And I'm supposed to find the heart of the Mountain and the breath of the Water."

"For Sun and Moon."

"… and Gloks have something to do with all of it."

"Yes."

They sat in silence for a bit.

"What if I'm not ready?" Neddy whispered, as if saying it too loud would make it true.

"You don't think you're ready?"

"That's not what I said… it's not what I meant…. I don't know…. What if I'm not?"

"Nonetheless, you go."

"Why can't we wait until I'm sure I'm ready?"

"When will you know that?"

"It doesn't make sense," Neddy protested. "All the other Girls went when they were ready. The stars don't form a line until it's the right time – when the Girl is ready." She tossed a pebble over the cliff. It bounced a few times off some jutting rocks, then disappeared below them. "It's not fair."

"No one has said it's fair. It just *is*." Rebane looked at the girl. "You've known this time would come since your first day. There is no way to change it. Just as you might not feel ready to wake up, the sun still rises. You might not want to end a good day, but the evening still comes. You must retrieve the heart of the Mountain for Sun, and the breath of the Water for Moon. Grab your handful of dust, and return to the Galen Tower before the stars align."

"I might fail," the girl's voice was small.

"Yes, you could fail."

"What happens if I do?"

"Galen and the Galenwood will end. Sun and Moon will die. Water and Mountain will fall. Dark will return to power and the world that we know will cease to exist."

Neddy hid the tear in her eye. "What do I do?"

"You do not fail."

They sat in silence again for almost as long as before

"Did I ever tell you how Erda found her hero?" Rebane asked.

Neddy thought for a moment. "No, I don't think so."

"She was stuck in a bog," Rebane smiled at the memory.

"Erda? In a bog?"

"Yes, all the way to her armpits."

Neddy grinned. The Woman always seemed so perfect, and the image of her standing in muck was hard to believe – and very enjoyable. But the story had to be true because Rebane was telling it.

"She'd been following footprints, and not watching where she was going."

"She didn't see a thing like a bog?"

"Not until it was too late," Rebane said. "There she was. Stuck up to the knees. The bog was hungry, and so it rose. Thinking it could pull her to the bottom."

"How did it think it could eat a Galenor?"

"It was a bog. It didn't think," Rebane said. "It had risen up to her armpits, and Erda didn't know what to do. When along came a fox. A red fox, with a bushy tail." Rebane looked at Neddy, "a very intelligent fox."

"Aren't all foxes smart?"

"This one was smarter than most," Rebane said. "The fox talked to the bog. Distracted it. And while it was talking, the bog didn't notice that the fox was laying down sticks at the edge near the girl. The pieces of wood sunk down at Erda's feet, giving her something to stand on. When there was enough wood laid down, she was able to walk out of the bog and she didn't get eaten."

"What did the bog do?"

"Oh, it was angry! It tried to chase them, but – it was a bog. They don't move very fast."

"And then she brought the fox back as her hero?"

"Yes," said Rebane.

Neddy laughed. It was fun to think of Erda running with bog-muck all over her white dress. It wasn't that she disliked Erda. It was just that … Erda was so annoyingly… *flawless.*

The light behind them grew stronger. Soon, Sun would be peeking over the ridge.

Neddy stood up and straightened her dress.

"So," she said, "I'm to go down the river, find the man who dances under the tree when Moon's belly is full, collect Sun's heart and Moon's breath, find my hero, get dust from the sky, and come back here. And I'm to do all of that before the Ascension."

"That is your Quest."

"Rebane."

"Yes?"

"You've been a very good teacher."

"And you've been a reasonably good student."

Neddy smiled and turned. And made her way over the edge of the cliff.

~~~~~~

On his journey back into the deep of the Galenwood, where he would wait for Neddy's return, Rebane daydreamed of being a red fox.

Chapter Five: The River

Neddy clambered down the mountain, holding her body close to the steep side of the cliff. *It would be nice if there was a trail or something,* she thought. *You'd think at least one of the Girls before me would have come back to make one.* At the same time she realized she probably wouldn't come back to etch a path into the rocks either. After all, if she and all the ones before her had to do this, so could the next one.

More than once, the gravel broke loose and she grabbed at larger rocks to keep from rolling to the bottom. When she reached the base of the cliff, the beach sand was a welcome reprieve from the sharp stones and tiny cactuses that had ridden between her toes on the way down. The shallow water cooled the sting in her feet.

Neddy looked up to where the river sprayed out of the mountain in a waterfall. She looked downriver. On its surface, the water looked smooth, peaceful. But she knew there was a churning current underneath. A strong current that would pull her under with nearly no effort. It wouldn't kill her because a Galenor can't die. But it *would* hinder her Quest. She needed a better idea than swimming.

Maybe there's another way, she thought, and she climbed onto the largest boulder at the water's edge. "Friend River, can you help me?" she called out.

"Sht'puk," the river splashed as it spoke, "yesh, we will try."

"Can you tell me? Is there a way to go downriver besides swimming?"

"Sshhh-t'puk… Are you ashking ush a queshtion?"

"Yes. I asked if you could help me."

"You didn't ashk ussshhh…"

"Yes, I did….. I just did."

"Ohhh…. sssh-t'puk..," the river said, "you ashked the water that wash here before. You didn't ashk ush."

"Well," Neddy worked to keep her voice calm, "can you help me?"

"Of courshe...."

"Is there a way to go down river besides swimming?"

"I think she's ashking ush a question," the river said to itself.

"I asked if there's a way to do downriver besides swimming. Is there beach along the cliffs?"

"Who doehsn't shwim? Sssshhhhwater only sshhwimss...," the river giggled.

It's laughing at me, Neddy thought. She wasn't as practiced at this as the others. She'd watched the Crone in deep conversations with the water in the well near her cave. And Erda had conversations with the lake and pond nearly every day.

"You need a boat," came a cackle from overhead.

A crow circled over the river a few times, stretched out his wings and floated down to stand on the boulder, next to Neddy's feet. "Quaw... You'll never get an answer from the river. It's impossible."

"It *is* possible," Neddy said, "I've seen Erda and the Crone do it many times."

"Where?"

"At the well. And the lake... and the pond."

"Well, that's different," the crow said. "Those waters lie still. You're always talking to the same water. But the river," he pointed a black feather, like a finger, towards the water rushing by, "you're talking to different water all the time. The water you first talked to, it's way downstream now. The water that's here now wasn't here then."

Neddy considered this. "So what do I do?"

"You need a boat."

"Well, yes, a boat would be nice," Neddy couldn't hold back the exasperation. "You don't happen to see one nearby, do you?"

"Quaaawww… Those who need help," the crow gurgled, "should really try to be a bit nicer." He flapped his wings and moved to hop off the rock.

Neddy drew in as much air as her lungs could take, and then a little bit more. She let it escape until more than she had taken in was gone. Remembering Rebane's lessons, she counted her toes, and counted them again. "I'm sorry," she said with a voice that was a bit too sweet. "You are right. I do need a boat. It would be *very nice* to have one. But, as you can see, a boat is something that I do not have." She sucked in one cheek, holding back everything else her tongue wanted to say.

"You have a boat," the crow said, flapping his wings and tucking them back in. "You just haven't made it yet."

Did Rebane ever teach me how to build a boat? Neddy wished she'd paid more attention to the lessons.

"Or," the crow continued, "quaaww… you could just get one. You could be like me," he pointed a feathered thumb at his chest. "Just look around and find what you need. There's always something you can use." An angry titter of small-bird chatter rose from the reeds and bushes. The crow cawed angrily at the birds, then said to Neddy, "Don't listen to them!"

"He's telling the truth," a low voice floated from across the river. "For once."

The crow and Neddy looked up to see a goat perched on an impossibly small stone jutting from the rocky cliff.

"Greetings, Galenor," the mountain goat said with a nod, dipping her bearded chin. "You must be on your Quest?"

"Yes," Neddy answered, grateful for a sensible conversation.

"And you're stuck." The goat leaned her head back and scratched the nub of her tail with one tip of her very long horns.

Rebane had told Neddy about animals that could stand on the side of a cliff, but she hadn't been sure whether to believe it. She believed it now, and was full of questions. But she needed to focus on the situation at hand.

"Well…," she said.

"Because, unless you want to swim a long way in a very cold river with a very fast current, you have to find a way to traverse the waters."

The water in the river giggled.

"I suppose," the goat sniffed, "I *could* suggest that you walk the cliffs of these mountains. But, unfortunately, you do not have the proper feet."

Neddy was feeling a bit insulted. And irritated. She put her hands on her hips and pulled herself as tall as she could. "You *do* know that I am a from the Galenwood, don't you?"

The river giggled.

The crow preened.

The goat, nibbling at a tuft of grass, said, "What of it?"

"Well…," Neddy looked around, "you're not supposed to talk to me that way."

"What way?"

"Everyone shows respect to a Galenor of the Galenwood."

"Quaaw? They do?" said the crow.

"Everywhere Erda goes, trees and bushes clear a path and the grass smooths before her feet. When the Crone stands, all around her bows down," *a bit of an exaggeration,* Neddy thought, *but it sounds good.*

"In the Galenwood, right?" the goat said.

"Yes!" Neddy's arms dropped, but she still tried to stand taller than she was.

"Quaw!" the crow turned his head nearly backwards, his beady eyes darting back and forth. "I didn't know we were in the Galenwood."

"We aren't," said the goat.

"Well, we're close," Neddy protested. She reached out with her arms and pointed at the cliff. "It's right up there."

"True," the goat said. "It's *there*, and we're *here*."

"Quaaww… The rules are different out here."

The newly-arrived water in the river giggled.

Neddy clenched her fists. Several words came to mind – many more if she wanted to get creative – but the only one that found its way past to her mouth wasn't even a finished, or real, one.

"Oooo….!" She jumped off the boulder, stomped across the sand and plopped herself down on the sandy beach.

It was quiet for a bit of time that was either long or short depending on who you were and what you were thinking.

SLAP!

The startled crow flapped his wings, ruffling his feathers. Neddy jumped. The mountain goat stopped scratching her tail with her horn, and might have nearly lost her footing except that losing one's footing is something that mountain goats never do. The river stopped giggling and its surface smoothed.

SLAP! The beaver slapped her tail again. "Where are your manners?" she scolded. "She is the Girl from the Galenwood! She is a Galenor." The furry, rather sizeable creature – almost as tall as Neddy if it stood upright – walked from the shallow edge of the river, her flat tail making a wide trail, and stopped in front of the girl. "Please excuse them," she said. Her dark brown eyes looked directly into Neddy's. Her voice was deep and soothing. "But you do know… this is *not* the Galenwood. And you are not the Goddess." She looked over to the two other animals, letting out a small snarl. "Yet!"

An awkward silence hovered for a little longer than a was comfortable.

Neddy's fingers picked at the tiny nuggets of sand around her.

The mountain goat regurgitated and ate her breakfast again.

Tiny splashes tapped against the beach and made the reeds sway.

The crow swiveled his head on his boney, feather-covered neck and slowly lifted one foot, thinking this might be a good time to exit. The crow's other foot couldn't follow because the beaver's hand was wrapped tightly around it.

"Crow," said the beaver.

"Quaw?" If crows could squeak, it would have been a squeak.

"I believe you could help." The beaver looked to the goat and then the river. "In fact," she said, "all of you can."

The goat nearly choked on her cud. "Me? What can I do?"

"You can retrieve the crow's second nest from its crag in the rock," the beaver answered. "Right behind you."

"What?!" the crow squawked. "You can't do that! I need that!" Angry, panicked feathers puffed and flicked. The bird jumped and flapped, trying to escape from the beaver's grasp.

"She needs it more," the beaver said calmly.

The goat looked from the girl to the crow, then back to the girl.

"But the eagle might come!" the crow protested.

"Your nestlings are safe in your first nest," the beaver said, "you can spare your false one."

Chittering in the reeds, countless small birds cheered this course of events. It was about time someone stole from the crow for a change.

"Snag it with that horn of yours and give it a good toss," the beaver instructed the goat.

Shrugging her shoulders, the goat decided she really didn't care whether the crow's nest stayed in the rocks of the mountainside or not. She tipped her head back and speared into the shadow in a crag and, with a flick of her head, sent the nest hurtling into the hair and across the river. The crow winced as it bounced several times before it stopped, settling flat, right-side up, on the beach.

The beaver squeezed the crow's leg one more time for good measure, then gestured for Neddy to follow. "Come take a look," she said, walking upright to the nest.

Rebane had taught Neddy about the homes of different creatures, but she'd only paid enough attention to learn that some burrowed in the ground while others lived in trees. Some birds had bigger nests than others, and some burrows were larger. That, of course, made sense because the animals were all different sizes. Now, seeing the crow's nest, she started remembering some of the details the golem had tried to teach her.

Proudly, the crow strutted over and hopped onto the nest, tucking a stray twig back in place with the tip of his beak.

"They're really quite good at nest-building," the beaver said as Neddy came to stand next to her.

"I never knew they were this large…" Neddy's voice trailed behind her as she walked around the nest.

"We're big birds," the crow said, "and in a good year we can have many nestlings."

"And they need extra space for all the things they steal from other birds," added the beaver, followed by a chirruping cheer from within the reeds.

"It's so… solid," Neddy said, pushing on one side – gently at first, then with some force.

"Quaaw! Of course it is," the crow cawed indignantly. "We find the strongest twigs, even if it takes a day's flight. Roots and threads of twine hold it together." The crow cocked his head. "The bed is soft for the children… made of hair and leaves."

"Where are your children?" Neddy asked.

"Quaw… They're in the true nest."

"Crows make two nests," the beaver said.

"One for the family," said the crow. "One for the eagles."

"No one but the crow knows where the true nest is. This is the false nest – the decoy for the eagles." The beaver turned to Neddy. "Weren't you taught about any of this?"

Probably, Neddy thought.

~~~~~~

After some conscientious tidying up of the nest by the crow, Neddy was sitting on the soft leaves in its center as it floated downstream.

"If I happen to lose my balance, would you please be sure that I don't fall out?"

"We'll'sh let you know right away ifsh you do," the water splashed.

Neddy took what comfort she could from the answer, and thanked the river. There was plenty of room in the nest and she settled herself in for a long ride.

As she left the shore, the beaver hopped onto the boulder on the beach. "Remember," she barked at the water, "she's from the Galenwood. Don't go making waves or anything that'll make it rough for her."

The river giggled, but did calm down a bit.

The nest floated, carried with care along the current – a glassy path before it, even when chopped white waves swirled around the stones and hidden debris. Birds flew overhead, curiously watching. Sometimes they perched on the edge of the nest to chat with Neddy, keeping her company. Now and then, when the birds were gone, a fish would pop its head above the water to look at the girl floating in the nest, then swim below to tell its friends and laugh at the absurdity.

Neddy floated, and daydreamed, and chatted… and floated…. and floated…

The cliffs rose high over the sides of the river at first, as if guarding the water. But, eventually, they relaxed and slouched a bit. They became hills, still made of sharp rocks but not as sheer. Then they became mounds of hard dirt. Along the way, grasses and flowers managed to grow roots between crags and stones.

And Neddy floated… and floated…

~~~~~~

Waterlogged, the nest turned lazily in the back-current churn along the shelled beach, coming to a rest in the reeds that grew where the water didn't move.

Neddy was startled awake by the shrill discordance of childlike quacking.

"Mommy! What kind of bird is that?"

"That's not a bird," a motherly, yet stern, voice answered. "Come back over here with your brothers and sisters."

"If it's not a bird, why is it in a nest?" The ducklings paddled to their mother, huddling around her.

The topmost edge of the crow's nest rocked on the water's surface, precariously close to submerging. Neddy carefully leaned over the side. She looked around at the beach and water and soggy plants.

"Can you please tell me where I am?" Neddy asked.

Mother duck checked to make sure all her ducklings were behind her. "You're in the marshes."

"Why's she in a crow's nest?" one of her children quacked.

"I'm sure that's her business." Mother duck spoke to her children but kept her eyes on Neddy.

"Crow let me borrow it," Neddy said. She tried to move around in the nest, wondering how she might get to solid ground without sinking first. She tried to stand, straddling her legs across the bed, seeking balance.

"It's a two-legger!" one of the ducklings cried, sending its siblings into a quacking fluster.

"Crow?" The mother's eyes instinctively scanned the skies for the sometimes-predator. She stretched out her wings to cover her children from view.

"Up the river," Neddy said.

"From up in the gorge." A mallard with dark, glimmering green-blue-black feathers covering its neck and shoulders, glided toward them, his strong legs and wide-webbed feet silently paddling beneath him. "This is the girl in the nest that the mudhens were talking about."

"I thought that was just gossip," the mother kicked her underwater feet, gliding closer to the nest. Her children stayed behind her in a closely-huddled group. Mother and father had told them about crows and two-leggers.

"Well, normally you can't trust much that the mudhens say." Father duck kicked once and drifted closer to his ducklings. "But now and then what they say turns out to be true." Reaching the nest, he stretched his neck, inspecting its craftsmanship. "They said the crane told them and she's not known to spread rumors."

Neddy didn't want to interrupt, but feeling there was a pause in place, she asked. "Where is the marsh?"

"Here, silly!" This came from the huddled ducklings and was followed by tiny laughing quacks which immediately fell silent with a sideways glance from their father.

"You came from the gorge?" the drake asked, still judging the structure of the nest.

"I don't know what it's called," Neddy answered. "I walked from the Galenwood with Rebane, the golem, my teacher… until we reached cliffs over the river where it comes out of the mountain… and then –"

"You're from the Galenwood?" The father duck's webbed feet quickly back-paddled, away from Neddy.

"From the Galenwood?" Mother said. "You're the Galenor Girl?"

"It must be the Quest –" said Father duck.

"Already? It seems too soon."

Mother and father duck quacked back and forth, interrupting each other, until one of the children quacked loudly, "What's the Galenwood?"

Neddy felt all the pairs of birds' eyes on her.

"She's from the sacred wood," mother said. "The Galenwood. Mind your manners and don't stare."

Hushed, squeaking quacks whispered.

"What's a sacred wood?"

"I dunno!"

"Maybe it's that big driftwood that sank under the reeds."

"How would she come from that?"

"Why would she need a nest? She's not a bird."

"I dunno!"

Neddy watched the little birds. They reminded her of the ducklings back home and she felt a little homesick. "Really – " she said, then realized she should be talking to their parents if she wanted any questions answered, and turned to the mother and father. "I don't know where I am."

"You're downriver from the gorge, in the marshes."

"Yes, but – " she leaned forward, tipping the edge of the nest below the water's surface. She sat back quickly, but that only made it rock, and heave, back and forth. Water filled the soaked nest and, with a glub – no splash or ripple, just a glub – it sank into the mud. Taking Neddy with it.

The girl stood, water up to her elbows, arms stretched out over the water, feeling ridiculous. *If I'd known it was only this deep I could've gotten out a bit more gracefully,* she thought, although she knew it wasn't true. Grace wasn't one of her stronger skills.

The squeaking quacks started again, but this time not in a whisper.

"Look! She's standing in the water without floating."

"Where'd the nest go?"

"Back to that waterlogged driftwood. I told you it was scared!"

"Sacred. No scared."

"Maybe she is a bird."

"Yeah, like a crane."

"You think she'll eat a frog?"

"Hush!" Their mother swam into the huddle of ducklings, breaking up their chatter.

With slow, strong strokes, the father paddled and, calling over his shoulder, said "Follow me. The dry beach is over this way."

~~~~~~

Sitting on the sandy beach, Neddy told the ducks about her journey so far.

"I don't know how long I've been riding in the nest," she said. "I think the moon danced across the sky a few times. But I'm not sure."

The ducks looked at each other.

"I have to finish my Quest before the stars form their bridge. I need to find the old man who dances under the tree when Moon's belly is full. I have to find the heart of the Mountain and the breath of the Water…"

"I know she's speaking the universal language," father said to mother, "but I have no idea what she's talking about. Do you?"

"… and I have to find the Gloks!" Neddy ran out of breath.

"No," mother said. "I don't know what she's talking about either."

The ducklings had been waiting in a safe spot under the brush.

Not yet having to worry about the concerns of the world and survival, the baby ducks still had their imaginations. A tiny quack said, "We think we might know what she means."

And the ducklings all started quacking at once.

"The stars in the sky are lining up."

"And they're getting bigger."

"That probably means they're getting closer."

"Starry stars!"

"They're arriving!"

"The old man — I once heard a tortoise talking about some old man who dances under trees."

"I'll bet the old lady in the village can tell her!"

"What's a Glok?"

"I bet I know."

"What?"

"Glok sounds stinky, and I'll bet it's exactly what it sounds like."

"Ewwww...."

"Wait," Neddy said. "What old lady?"

"There's an old woman who lives in the village," father duck said. "She teaches the children. Cares for the ones who've got no one else."

"How do I find the village?"

Chapter Six: The Village

Neddy sat under a tree that grew at the top of a hill that sloped down to the village. She knew it wasn't a Galenwood tree, but thought she'd try asking it anyway. *You never know until you try*, she thought.

"Can't *you* tell me where the old man is?" she asked.

A breeze made some of the leaves flutter, but otherwise the branches were silent.

"But I've never been to a village. How am I supposed to find my way around?"

The leaves, branches and tree remained silent.

"And with all those people down there, I'm supposed to find an old woman who can help me?"

Nothing.

"Ugh!"

She'd spent a day and a half walking from the marshes to this hill, following the ducks' instructions. The humans' village, they'd told her, was on the same side of the river as the marsh, which was the opposite side from the Galenwood. The path she followed hadn't really been a path at all, but more a series of landmarks to find and pass. The ducks hadn't travelled it themselves, but they'd flown over the land. Mother and father duck took turns with the directions:

"Follow the edge of the reeds until they stop."

"Keep away from the willows. There's sticker bushes inside there."

"There's sand dunes where the reeds stop."

"Like beach sand, but they go away from the water."

"When you get to the dunes, look for a big rock at the far end."

"You can't miss it. Across the dunes, where the sand stops."

"Walk towards the rock."

"And when you get there, the sand turns to gravel and then grass."

"Walk towards the hills."

"It'll take you a while."

"Took us only a few minutes."

"She's not flying."

"Oh. Right. Yes, it'll take you a while."

"Stay on the tops of the hills as much as you can. Eventually
– "

"You'll start seeing smoke."

"Eventually you'll be seeing smoke. From chimneys."

"Humans build houses, and then build fires inside of them."

"Humans are strange."

"And that's where the village is."

~~~~~~

The sun was below the horizon before Neddy reached the end of the reeds and the beginning of the dunes. It had risen again, not quite as bright as the day before, on the other side of the world by the time she got to the rock. It was setting again when she saw the chimney smoke. A few times, when she couldn't see her way in the sand or when she was in the dips between hills, she'd asked the gravel and sand to show her the way. Sometimes they did, and eventually she reached the tree on the hill that sloped up to overlook the village. She decided to wait until morning before going down the hill into where the humans lived, remembering how Rebane had told her that humans were suspicious of anything that walked their streets in the dark.

Neddy didn't want to go into the village. Rebane had described villages, towns and cities – but it wasn't until now that she began to grasp the picture her teacher had tried to paint. There was what looked like a main road going down the center, lined with buildings like boxes on either side. Every three of four boxes, a smaller road broke off from the main and made its way between more, but smaller, boxes. It looked kind of like the branch of a tree, if the branch was straight and flat and the twigs grew straight out at right angles and if the leaves were square and evenly spaced along the branch and twigs. Offshoots of road spindled away from the village's crowded center, going to homes that lined the outskirts. She decided what it really looked like was a big, unpleasant dandelion.

Neddy had learned the facts from Rebane – houses, roads, shops and inns – but the Crone had told her the things that were the reason why she was hesitant:

Humans clustered together for safety from dangers they themselves created.

They didn't know – had long ago forgotten – how to listen to the earth. How to talk to Water and Mountain. They didn't remember the universal language nor that there even was such a thing.

They feared what they called "wild" and shuttered themselves away from the voices of the wind.

They hid from Sun and Moon.

They wore shoes.

Neddy watched the village wake up. One by one, chimneys exhaled gray then black smoke. People stepped through doors, in and out of their boxes. It was quiet at first, but one voice added to another and another until a hum buzzed in the background of everything.

She heard a loud *clang!* and a clatter and a voice rose above the others, shouting short words that didn't sound happy.

A poof of dust rose from somewhere in the midst of the crowded place.

A black dot rose in the air and grew wings, and a bundle of something gray ran through the dirty streets. Both moved quickly away from the ruckus and towards the outer edges of the village.

The crow flew high into the air, and the dog half-chased, half-followed the bird. Neddy watched them run towards her hill. The dog stopped when he saw her and wuffed under his breath. One ear stood at attention while the other tried to get past its permanent half-flop. A small ridge formed along his back, albeit barely visible under the coarse chaos of dirty gray hair.

"There's someone on that hill," he said to the crow, with a little bit of snort and growl added to accentuate the potential significance.

"I know," the crow cawed back, "I've been following her. Come on, I'll introduce you."

"Is she… *safe?*"

"She's one of the few two-leggers you *can* trust."

"As much as I can trust you?" The dog cocked his head sideways and squinted at the bird.

"No," the crow laughed. "you can't trust me at all," and he swooped down, showing off with a couple of spirals, and landed on the ground in front of Neddy.

"Girl of the Galenwood…" the crow said, bowing his head low. Neddy wasn't sure if the honor was sincere.

The crow walk-hopped to Neddy's side and watched the dog cautiously stepping his way closer.

"Girl, dog. Dog, Girl," the crow said, pointing with a feather-tip between the two. Then, to Neddy, he said, "He showed up while I was breakfasting. Nice enough. Decent manners."

"Breakfasting?"

"Yes. What?"

"Where?"

"Back of a restaurant – that's where human people go to eat. You can't be too choosy." The bird ruffled his feathers and preened them back in place with his pointy black beak. "Not bad eating." Finished with the grooming, he turned to the dog. "Up until that two-legger came out and chased us off. Right?"

"Nice to meet you," Neddy said to the dog.

"Likewise."

"Do you have a name?"

"A name?"

Crow snickered.

"What?" Neddy asked.

"Humans call me all sorts of things. But I don't have a *name*."

"How do others know you?"

"Quaaww…" The crow laughed, and said "Yes, dog. How do others know you?"

"They smell me."

"Oh," Neddy said.

"We all smell different," said the dog. "It's how I know you. I can smell the Galenwood on you. And you've been around…. ducks… a beaver… a goat? Hmmm….. there's lots of smells all over you."

"You know the Galenwood?"

"Anyone who's not human knows the Galenwood."

Neddy thought about this for a moment, then returned to the question at hand. "But how do I know you?"

"You can smell me, if you like." The dog turned to face away from the girl. "Right there under the tail is usually the best place."

"Ummm…" Neddy nudged the dog's hind end away from her face, "that's okay. How about if I call you Dog?"

"You wouldn't be wrong with that."

"Okay. I'm Neddy."

"Do you have a name for the bird?" Dog asked.

"Not that I've thought of yet…." Neddy looked sideways at the crow. "Not one that's polite."

"I think *Crow* has a nice ring to it," said the crow.

They sat quietly for a while, watching the town wake up.

Neddy broke the silence. "Are you following me, Crow?"

"Yes," Crow answered, "You owe me a nest."

Neddy stood up, brushing small rocks and dirt off her dress. She considered the crow for a minute, then decided not to tell the bird what had happened to his nest.

"I have to go to the village and find an old woman," she said. "You want to come along?"

"I'll wait here," Dog said, "if it's all the same to you. I've had enough kicking and yelling for one day already."

"Me too," Crow added.

"I don't know how long I'll be."

"That's okay. We'll be here."

Neddy started down the slope of the hill, but stopped when the dog called after her.

"Look for some children," Dog said. "There's an old woman that takes care of lost kids. They can probably show you where she is." Dog turned to Crow and added, "They pet me and give me cookies."

"Thank you," Neddy said, and turned towards the village.

"There used to be a boy," said Dog, watching the girl go. "I would see him a lot behind the butcher's shop. He didn't have a real name either, and he was always talking about frogs." Dog lay down. "I've not seen him for a while. But I'm sure I smelled him on the girl. Something makes me think he's happier now than ever before."

~~~~~~

Old man! Old man! Under the tree.
Dancin', dancin', crazy as can be.

Arms to the sky,

Jumpin' up and down,

Crazy old man jumps down into the ground!

Neddy heard the chanted rhyme and laughter long before finding the children. She watched them hitting an old wooden barrel with sticks until it fell over and a boy crawled out, laughing harder than any of the rest. Then they set the barrel upright and began the chant again.

Old man! Old man! Under the tree.

Dancin', dancin', crazy as can be.

Arms to the sky,

Jumpin up and down,

Crazy old man jumps down into the ground!

As they sang, they danced around the barrel, taking turns to hit it with their sticks. On the last word, the girl whose stick was on the barrel last scrambled into it and all the other children commenced to hitting it, laughing and jumping around and over each other, until the barrel fell over again and the girl crawled out.

Neddy watched them do this several times before the words to the chant registered something in her. *Old man under a tree!* she exclaimed inside her head. She carefully made her way towards the group.

Neddy's first day had been long before anyone in this village had been born, but since she looked close to the ages of the children she decided to see if they could help her. When they saw her, the children stopped singing and stood, sticks in hands, warily watching her approach.

"Hello," Neddy said, trying to smile as nicely as she could.

The children stared.

"My name is Neddy."

The children stared.

"The dog said I should find you."

"The dog?" one of them said.

"Yes."

"The dog talked?"

"Yes....?"

In an eruption of laughter, somebody cried out, "She must be crazier than the old man!"

Neddy mentally scolded herself for forgetting that humans didn't know about the universal language. She waited until the laughing stopped.

"I need to find an old woman," she said.

A girl stepped out in front of the group. Her clothes were like the others', too big in some places, too small in others, and looked like they might have been clean a day or so ago. She stood, hands on her hips, feet spread apart as a guard might do, and said, "Why's your hair like that?"

"Like what?"

"All messy."

"Uh…. that's how it grows?"

"Mine does, too. But I gots a brush. Don't you got a brush?"

"I don't know…." Neddy tried to remember if Rebane had told her anything about humans and their hair. "My hair does what it wants to do," she said. "Can you tell me where the old woman is?"

"Which old woman?"

It dawned on Neddy that, unlike the Galenwood, there might be more than one old woman. "I'm told she takes care of kids," she said.

The girl didn't answer, but turned to confer with the other children. They whispered back and forth, taking turns to look at the newcomer. They seemed to come to some sort of agreement, and the lead girl turned back to Neddy, resuming her hands-on-hips-feet-spread-apart position.

"Why do you need to see her? Are you lost or something?"

Neddy decided not to tell the children about the golem, the Galenwood, her being a Girl soon to be a Goddess, and certainly not about the Quest. So she nodded. "Yes."

The girl's stance eased a little, and she looked over her shoulder. "What do you think?"

"We can surround her," a boy somewhere in the group said, "like we do when we play soldiers, and march her there."

The bunch of heads nodded, and the girl turned back to Neddy. "Come on. We'll take you there."

The group of urchins formed a circle around Neddy and, with the lead girl in front, marched in place until their feet found unison, and moved forward down the alleyway of dirt.

~~~~~~

Being surrounded by escorts, Neddy couldn't see very well where they were going. But she could tell they were following a road that led away from the center of the town. It was packed dirt, narrow here, wide there, with grasses growing where carts and feet didn't travel. Eventually they came to a low fence made of stone with a gate of woven sticks. Feathers hung from the gate and Neddy wasn't sure if they were put there by someone, or if they were the remnants of some unfortunate event. In the yard inside the fence, cows and geese mingled freely.

The group opened to a half-circle so Neddy was standing at the gate.

"Hullo?" the lead girl called out. "Are you home?"

The gate opened. Neddy was sure she didn't see anyone touch it, but decided she was wrong. This wasn't the Galenwood.

Neddy took care not to step on the flowers, or what some people might call weeds, that grew haphazardly among small clumps of low grass, as the children led her through the yard up a short path of flat stones and to the steps of a stone porch attached to a house also made of stone. A thatched roof covered it all, interrupted by a stone chimney with a small stream of dark gray smoke wisping from it. When they reached the door, it opened.

Light sifted through gauze-curtained windows into a large room, the only room in the cottage, illuminating the dust and fibers floating in the air. A kitchen and table were on one side of the room, several beds on the other, and a very comfortable-looking chair surrounded by pillows and small stools on a woven-rag rug in front of the fireplace. In a chair at the table, peeling potatoes, was an old woman. She didn't get up, and when the children entered, she slid a bowl of unpeeled tubers to the center of the table along with a small basket of paring knives. The children sat on benches that circled the table, each picking up a knife and potato, and began peeling. An empty seat was left for Neddy so that she would be sitting directly opposite of the woman.

Nobody spoke for a while, which gave Neddy time to look around. Herbs hung, drying, from hooks in the ceiling. On the walls were more hooks, some with towels, others with pairs of candles joined by a single wick lashed across the dowel, and others with assortments of dried flowers and leaves and twigs.

Neddy sat and looked across the table. The woman was old, but it was hard to tell just how many years she'd experienced. Gray hair wound into a thick bun on top of her head, and if wrinkles were years she'd be more than a hundred. Her fingers, though gnarled, were quick and agile.

"Are you going to just sit there, or are you going to help out?" The woman asked, not looking up from her knife and spud. Her old, nimble fingers peeled potato after potato, sometimes keeping its skin in one piece. The children tried to do the same without much success but having fun nonetheless.

Never having the need to eat, Neddy had never peeled a potato – or any other fruit or vegetable, for that matter. But it didn't look too difficult. She'd etched runes into wood and stone. A potato shouldn't be hard at all. Choosing a medium-sized one from the bowl, she picked up a knife. The first thing she cut was her own thumb. It wasn't on purpose.

"She cut herself," the boy next to her said, gasping a little bit and trying to get a better look. "She's not bleeding! Where's the blood?"

Neddy held her thumb up in front of her face, thinking *of course there's no blood*. Then she looked around the table and saw that, to the other children, this must not be normal.

"Wrap this around it," the woman said, tossing a small, clean rag across the table, and resumed the peeling of potatoes.

"Where did you find this one?" the woman asked, not to anyone in particular.

"In the alley," the girl who had been the leader said. "We were playing *Old Man* and she came outta nowhere."

The girl sitting closest to Neddy stared at the injured, unbleeding thumb.

"Out of nowhere, you say…" said the woman.

"Yeah," a boy sitting nearer the woman said, "and she said she was looking for an old woman –"

"So we brought her here," the lead girl finished.

"Where are you from?" the woman asked.

The woman still didn't look up, but Neddy knew this question was for her. She thought for a minute, not sure how much to say.

"I'm from the woods…?"

"You don't sound so sure," the woman said.

"I'm sure. I'm from the woods."

"Which woods," the woman asked. She'd stopped peeling and was looking at Neddy now.

Neddy looked around the table. "The Galenwood."

Somebody snickered, "the Galenwood's not real."

"Yes it is," Neddy protested. *I live there with a golem and Erda and the Crone and lots of trees and animals that I can talk to…* was on the tip of her tongue, but she kept it there.

"Why do you say that?" the woman asked the one who'd snickered.

"It's just a fairy tale."

"Well, my young ones," the woman put her knife to the potato again, "I'm sorry to tell you this, but the Galenwood is a real place." She peeled for a bit while everyone waited for her to say more. Then she stopped, put the potato and knife on the table, wiped her hands on the skirt of her dress and said, "Do you children know who the Goddess of Galen is?"

Nobody answered.

The woman gestured to Neddy. "This is a Goddess. Well, she *will* be. Soon enough."

Still, nobody spoke.

"Her thumb doesn't bleed because she's not human," said the old woman.

"Nuh-uh…!" one of the boys said.

"What is she?" said a small girl whose nose barely peeked over the table, and who was more willing to believe. "A fairy?"

"No," the woman said. "She's more than that…."

By now everyone had stopped peeling their potatoes and everyone was looking at Neddy.

"Do you have wings hidden somewhere?" one of them asked, leaning to peek behind Neddy.

"No," Neddy answered.

"Can you shapeshift?" a boy asked. He'd heard about shapeshifters and wasn't sure whether he should be worried.

"No."

Many more questions were asked, most of them all at the same time, and a flurry of absolutely-known-for-sure information was exchanged. Neddy lost track and stopped trying to answer. She looked across the table to the old woman, who was smiling with crow's feet that reminded her of the old crone's lammergeier.

"Well, now…" the woman said, and the chattering stopped. "You were looking for an old woman. You found me…" She winked at the children. "What did you need to find me for?"

"I'm supposed to find an old man who dances under a tree. The ducks said I should come to the village, and the dog said I should look for an old woman – and I guess that's you… maybe – and then I heard them singing about an old man, so I thought they might be able to help me, so I asked them."

"She talks to dogs *and* ducks!" Giggles rounded the table.

"Is that because you're a Goddess?"

Neddy looked to the woman. "Can you help me?"

"Why are you looking for the old man?"

"I think he's going to help me." Neddy paused. Once again she was unsure how much she should say. How much of this should be kept secret? Any of it? None of it? But she needed help. And the old woman *did* know about the Goddess of Galen. She decided. "I'm looking for the breath of the Water and the heart of the Mountain. The Gloks took them from Moon and Sun, and I'm pretty sure the old man is supposed to be able to help me."

The woman looked around the table.

"Children," she said, "you are never to tell anyone what you're about to hear." Old eyes locked with each child, one at a time. "Is there anyone here who can't keep a secret? Because if you can't you'll need to go and sit outside on the porch. Right now."

Nobody moved.

"Hmmm...," the woman straightened her back. Neddy heard cracking coming from the aged spine. "Well... Okay then."

The woman gathered her thoughts for a moment, and the children around the table leaned forward, eager for another of the woman's stories. She had so many, and whether they involved goblins or unicorns, witches or fish, they were always fun to listen to.

"The old man, the one that you children dance and sing about, is one of the Keepers who watch over the world when the Goddess can't be there, which is almost all of the time."

"But —" Neddy started.

"Now, no interruptions," said the woman. "Just listen."

"Yeah, shhh!" said one of the boys at the table. "Just listen!"

The woman smiled at the boy, then at everyone around the table.

"The Goddess can't be everywhere. Nothing wrong in that, you see. It's just a matter of fact. How is one person supposed to see everything everywhere all around the world?"

"She can sense things," Neddy answered.

"True... true," said the woman. "But sensing from a distance isn't the same as being there and seeing it. Now, after a while, the different places around the world got a little bit tired of being on their own, so they started making their own guardians. The *Keepers*. The old man is a Keeper of the desert where he lives. There are others for every desert. There's a Keeper for every ocean and lake and stream. Everywhere in the world, there's a Keeper watching over it."

"Are they like the Goddess?" one of the children asked.

"Yes... and no. They're the same because, like the Goddess, they're very old. Some are older than others because the place that they watch is older, but they are all older than any human. The *difference*, however, is that they don't change. There is no Ascension. A Keeper is made once, for a specific place, and they live there and never die."

"Why wasn't I taught about the Keepers," Neddy wondered aloud.

"Maybe you were, maybe you weren't." The old woman smiled. "And you probably don't know when you've met one."

Neddy thought for a moment. "So," she said, "I'm going to meet a Keeper?"

"As a matter of fact, you already have. You're talking to one now." The woman looked at the wide eyes around the table. "Like I told you," she said, "the world created a Keeper wherever there was a need. And, one thing is certain, every city, village, town... any time there's a community of people – humans, that is – there's a need for someone to take care of those that are set aside." She smiled at the boys and girls seated around the table. "In every one of those places, you'll find someone like me. Someone who takes care of the children, the poor, the ones who have no one else to watch out for them."

"I *knew* you was old!" a small girl, the one who still believed in fairies, whispered.

"Yes, I am old. I'm as old as this village, and I'll keep getting older and older the longer the village is here. Likely, I'll still be here if and when this place becomes a town, and then a city. Because there will always be a need."

"And the old man?" said Neddy.

"Oh, he's much, much older than me. He's as old as the desert. And I think the desert has been here... Oh my," she looked at the children, "how old would you say the desert's been here?"

"For*ever!*" said one of the older girls.

"Does he really dance under a tree when Moon's belly is full?" asked one of the boys.

The woman laughed. "Yes, he does. He's peculiar in that way. But," she said, serious again, "he's likely not to be doing that for much longer. You say Moon had its breath stolen. Without its breath, Moon can't fill its lungs. Can't go full and round. No more full belly for the old man to dance under."

"I know I don't have much time," said Neddy. "Can you tell me how to find him?"

"Go back to where your dog and bird are waiting for you," the woman winked knowingly, "Look towards the mountains and keep walking until you come to the desert. You'll find the old man there."

"Sounds simple enough," said Neddy.

"Hmmm… it does, doesn't it?" The woman got up from her chair and went to where an assortment of bags and pouches hung on hooks set into the wall near the wash basin.

"Being from the Galenwood, you might not need to eat, but the dog does." The woman chose a pouch about the size of Neddy's hand. On one side it had a sun embroidered against a blue sky, and a moon embroidered against an indigo night on the other. Then she took a soft, wide-mouthed flask that was hanging on another hook and, handing it to Neddy, said, "He'll be needing water, too."

Neddy hadn't thought about these things. "Thank you," she said.

"Don't worry about the crow," the woman added. "It won't need any help."

The woman wrapped an arm around Neddy's shoulders and nudged the girl towards the door and out onto the porch. She said, "Remember what you've been taught and you'll be fine."

Neddy stood at the top of the stone steps for a few minutes. It dawned on her that she hadn't told the old woman about the crow, nor that Crow and Dog were waiting for her. *How did she know?* she wondered. She considered knocking on the door and asking, but knew she probably wouldn't get an answer and besides, she probably *had* said something and just didn't remember.

She stuck the flask and pouch into a pocket, left the porch, and made her way back to the sloping hill on the outskirts of the village.

Chapter Seven: The Desert

"**S**o, where to next?" Crow asked.

Dog sensed the pouch of biscuits and was snuffling the skirt, trying to find where it was hidden.

Neddy stood, looking at the town. It had been neither as wondrous nor as frightening as she'd been led to believe. Or, rather, as she had led herself to believe. She shook her head. A cluster of red hair fell into her face. And she wondered... *what's a brush?*

"Quaaww..." Crow croaked, clearing his throat.

Neddy turned away from the town and, hands on her hips, surveyed the land on the opposite side of the hill. It looked inviting from where she stood. But beyond the grassy hills, in the direction away from the river, was a desert, and she remembered Rebane's lessons about that kind of place. She knew it was made up of rocks – dark, sunbaked rocks – and that there would be gullies carved into it by years of rain. Her Quest wasn't going to get any easier. Not for a while.

"I'm supposed to find an old man who dances under a tree. He does it when Moon's belly is full."

"When will that be?"

"Not long."

"Maybe it's just me," Crow said, "but that's a desert in front of us. Lots of cactuses, maybe a few bushes, but not too many trees."

Neddy pointed across the expanse. "She said to start walking and he'll find us."

"How far?"

"She didn't say."

"Did she say anything about giving me something to eat?" Dog was still snuffling the skirt.

Neddy pulled out the pouch and gave Dog a few biscuits. She put the bag back in the pocket, and started walking.

~~~~~~~

Neddy scrambled up another gully, rocks and dirt giving way and offering almost nothing solid to push a foot against. She felt like she'd won a battle when she reached the top, but lost that feeling when she looked across at the plateau. The only thing that broke the never-ending flatness was an occasional dry and scraggled bush or a cactus.

"I don't think we're getting anywhere," she said. "It seems like every time we go down a gully and come back up again we're in the same place we started."

Crow circled overhead, calling down, "I don't see any trees."

"There *has* to be," Neddy huffed. With determination she marched across the rocks, stepping around the jagged ones and over the ones that hadn't yet been worn down small. She slid and scrambled down the side of the next gully and made her way across the trail left by a river from some long-ago rain. The dry riverbed alternated soft sand with debris caught in an old current. Once across the gully's wash, she made her way up the other side. Reaching the top, she walked across the flat, dark stones to the next gully and did it all over again.

Sun was high above and the only shadows were the ones directly underfoot. Neddy was frustrated. She gave Dog a biscuit and some water, using the large cap of the flask as a bowl.

Crow landed on a jagged rock next to her. He didn't have anything to say, and that made Neddy glad. She closed her eyes and tried to make her mind go blank. Dog finished his snack and, as dogs will do when nothing interesting is happening at the moment, decided to take a nap.

They'd been climbing up and down gullies, across plateaus, and back into gullies again for several days. Each day, Neddy noticed, there was a bit less sunlight. Each night, after drawing a circle of protective sigils for them to sleep in, she watched as Moon was unable to fill its lungs. The first night of her journey, when she was floating down the river, Moon was round and full. Then it waned. That wasn't unusual. When Moon exhaled, emptying its lungs of Water's breath, it always grew thin. But then, when Moon was supposed to grow as it inhaled the breath, it only reached halfway before waning again. Moon hadn't had a full belly, hadn't been round, since she'd left the Galenwood. Neddy worried, but kept it to herself. *No need*, she thought, *to make Dog and Crow worry, too.* She tried not to think about what might happen, what would be lost, if she couldn't find the breath or the heart. If she couldn't save Moon and Sun.

Eyes closed, Neddy tried to sense anything that might tell her where the old man might be. A small breeze kept the air cool and made the small tufts of grasses rustle. She could hear clods of dirt breaking apart in gullies, falling in small avalanches to the bottoms of the hills. Rodents dug holes. Bugs crawled on cactuses. Spiders wove webs between the branches of shrubs. Dog rumbled a low growl. Rocks and pebbles shifted, rolling against each other. *Wait… why is dog growling?*

"Qwwaaaa…" Crow croaked quietly, and whispered, "we have company."

Opening one eye just a sliver, Neddy saw a lizard laying on a low slab of stone in front of her. It was the color of desert dirt, with a wide mouth and a long tail that twitched at the tip. It blended so well with its surroundings, she wondered if it had been there all along.

Crow eyed the lizard and would have licked his lips if he had any.

The lizard blinked it's dirt-colored lids over black beady eyes. "Who are you?"

Neddy sat up, straightening her back, "I'm Neddy – "

"No," the lizard interrupted, "*Who* are you?"

The girl looked at the lizard, the crow, the dog, then the lizard again.

"My name is – "

This time Crow interrupted her. "She's Galenor Nedrick of the Galenorae."

"People call me Neddy," Neddy said, looking at Crow and wondering how he knew her full name.

Crow tilted his head toward the girl and said, "I'm a crow. We know things."

"Galenor Neddy…," the lizard said, its narrowed eyes fixed on the girl.

"Why is she here?" A voice came from behind Neddy, and she turned to see another lizard. It was a bit smaller than the first.

"The stars must be lining up again," this voice was lower and came from a rock to Neddy's left. "She's on her Quest."

Neddy stopped looking, and instead she *saw*. Lizards surrounded them on all sides. Most were tannish-brown with speckles from the tip of their nose to the end of their tail. Some were more greenish or red than the others. A few were gray and thick and had no tail. Some looked fresh and young, while others had skin that had seen many summers. They all stared at her with puddle-black eyes.

Dog stopped growling and whispered to Neddy, "They're everywhere…."

Crow tried to count their numbers, but lost count and decided to look for which one would be the juiciest instead.

"Don't even think about it…," one of them hissed at the bird.

Crow looked up and around then turned to preen himself, pretending not to know what the lizard was talking about.

"What's a Galdenoradid?" one of the small green lizards asked. A group of identical lizards around it giggled.

"He's right isn't he?" the first lizard said. "Is it the Quest?"

Feeling slightly overwhelmed, Neddy's tongue shrunk to the bottom of her mouth. She nodded.

"She's probably looking for the old man," it was the low-voiced one again.

A tiny lizard, no longer than Neddy's smallest finger, hopped onto the girl's foot. "Then why's she up here?" Neddy curled her toes, hoping the little thing wasn't thinking of running up her leg.

"She'll never find him up here." This was from another voice somewhere among the rocks.

Neddy gave up trying to see who was talking. Addressing the first lizard, she asked, "Do you know where I might find him?"

"Follow the wash," said the deep voice. "He lives in caves in the gullies."

"But the woman said I need to cross the desert – "

"Never mind that. You *will* be crossing the desert. Just down in the gullies instead of up on top."

"Which gully do I follow?"

"Doesn't matter," the first lizard said. "They all lead to the same place."

"Where?"

"To where he wants to find you."

Neddy stood up and looked across the desert. "But –"

She turned.

The lizards were gone.

She looked at Crow. "Are you sure you can't just fly up and see where he is?"

"No." Crow ruffled his feathers. "I've looked a dozen times every day we've been out here. He's nowhere to be found."

"I'd try to sniff him out," Dog offered, "but everything around here just smells like dirt to me. It's like it's all up in my nose." The dog snorted.

"Well, then," Neddy said, "I suppose we need to get down into a gully."

~~~~~~~

Neddy couldn't tell how low the sun was. What had begun as a wash in a gully had become a ravine with tall sides that blocked her view of the horizon.

From the upper, flat land of the desert the gullies all looked the same. But, as it turned out, some were wide, some were narrow, some were sandy, some were rocky, some had tiny cactuses that got caught in Dog's coat. Neddy and Dog walked, following the dry rivulets in the sand that showed which way the water had run long ago. Gullies blended into each other like tributaries, growing wider and deeper. Along the sides of the dry walls of the ravine were holes – nesting places either made by erosion or claws or both. Some of the holes were smaller than Neddy's hand. Others were big enough that she and Dog could have taken a nap at their doorstep with plenty of room left for Crow to have a look around.

"Did you hear that?" Dog asked, looking over his shoulder.

"I don't hear anything but our crunching feet." Neddy said, "But...," she stopped and looked behind them, "I do feel eyes on us."

"There's nobody around but us, that I can see," said Crow, spiraling down from a low flight and landing on Dog's back.

Dog reached back, nipping at the bird. "Get! Off!" Dog shook his body, violently. "I've told you. You can't ride on me."

Crow held on, his talons grabbing Dog's scruffy coat. "Aw, come on…. I just want a little rest…"

"No!" Dog dropped and rolled in the dirt, forcing the bird off.

"Qwaaaaawwww…." Crow grumbled. He hopped a few paces alongside Neddy, then, making a show of it, flapped his wings and flew ahead to a rock they'd reach fairly soon.

Neddy thought about saying something about crows and what they had in common with things that are annoying, but she decided not to and continued walking.

A poof of dirt floated into the air as Dog got up, shook himself and trotted to catch up with the girl.

"I know something's there," Dog growled, turning his head sharply from side to side, looking all around them.

Neddy looked around. Then she looked up. "Those are the colors of the setting sun," she said. "We should start looking for a place to spend the night." And she thought, *my legs feel a bit weak and my feet are aching.* It was a new sensation for her. She knew Dog was probably tired from so much walking, but Galenorae didn't get tired and she wasn't sure how to feel about the new development.

They found a cave tucked into the wall of the ravine that looked safe from collapsing in on them. It was above the watermark of the highest rivers brought by past rain – not that there was any chance of rain today – but still an easy climb. By the looks of it, they weren't the first ones to come to rest in this spot.

Crow peered into the mouth of the cave. "Are you sure nothing's gonna come out of this at night?"

"No," Neddy said, smoothing the dirt around them. She needed a large enough circle for them to sleep inside the ring of sigils she'd be drawing.

"Is that a *no* you're not sure or a *no* nothing's gonna come out?" Crow was still looking into the dark cavity. "Birds can't smell, and I'm not one of those ones that can see in the dark," he said, "but I'm sure I hear... things... rustling around in there."

"I don't smell anything," Dog said. "Any chance it's time for another biscuit?"

Crow scooted into the ring before Neddy drew the last sigil and closed the circle of protection.

Chapter Eight: The Old Man

Neddy was surprised when the morning light woke her. Not because it was morning, but because she'd been asleep. It was another strange feeling – sleeping – among others she'd had since leaving the Galenwood. Yesterday she was *tired* and her feet *hurt*. Last night she *slept*. And now… *is this what hungry feels like?*

A soft, wet nose in her ear let the girl know Dog was awake and restless. Crow was still asleep and squawking something to himself under his breath. Neddy reached out to smooth the dirt over a sigil, breaking the protective circle, and Dog bounded out to explore the cave.

Curious, Neddy took one of Dog's biscuits from the bag, nibbled one of its rough edges, then gobbled down the rest of it. Having heard the rustle of the opening pouch, Dog came back and nudged her. She took out a couple more biscuits and poured some water into the lid of the flask. She thought of having another one, and *this other thing…. what is it… am I thirsty?* Thinking about these new sensations of needing to eat and drink, she decided they weren't something she wanted to linger. *But*, she thought, *I shouldn't drink it all up. Dog will… we will need it later.* She looked into the pouch. *That's odd,* she thought. The pouch was as full of biscuits as it had been when the old woman had given it to her. The flask was full, as well. *How…?* No matter. She was hungry and thirsty. She ate and drank until *…so this is what it feels like to be full.*

For the first time since her first day, Neddy truly understood why animals slept and why they grazed, hunted, collected and stored food, and why they gathered at the edges of waters.

Neddy pulled herself up to sit and face the ravine. The sun was rising from behind her and she watched the morning gray crawl across the rocks and sand to find places to hide from its light. A long shadow, cast by the wall that held her cave, crept across the wash to the base of the cliff, up the side of the ravine and towards her feet. As it moved, the ground behind it was washed with weak yet warm sunlight that made its way to the girl. She watched the light cross the circle of sigils, up the sides of the cave and into its mouth.

"What's this?" Neddy said when she saw the cave's entrance. Scrambling to her feet, she stumbled the few steps to where runes were carved into the rock, framing the dark, deep mouth of the cave. She ran her fingers over the signs. They looked familiar... and as her hands brushed the markings, a low vibration turned into a hum. A tune she almost knew. Like hearing a foreign language that shared its roots with yours. She wished again that she had paid more attention to Rebane's lessons.

Muttering something unintelligible, Crow woke up. Muttering something else about sunlight, he tried to hide his face behind black-feathered wings. "Quaaaww...," he grumbled, giving up. "I was having a fairly good dream about lizards and –" Crow saw the runes. "I *told you* there's something in there."

"How do you know something's in there?" Dog asked.

"Look!" A long black feather pointed at the symbols etched into the rock wall. "It says so right there!"

"You can read this?" Neddy asked.

"Of course I can," Crow answered. "It's written in the universal tongue. "

Dog looked at Neddy. Neddy bit her lower lip. *I should have been able to read it!* she thought.

"I never learned to read," Dog said. "What does it say?"

Crow's beak moved as he silently read the runes. When done, the bird turned to Neddy and Dog. "It says this is someone's cave. Somebody named Karboney. And it says to stay out."

"Does it really say to stay out?" Dog asked, looking around the bird's shoulder to where the writing was.

"Well," Neddy said, brushing dirt from the skirt of her dress, noticing that there were a few spots that wouldn't leave, "let's go." And she walked towards the entrance that the runes surrounded.

"Wait a minute!" Crow squawked.

Dog four-legged-skipped behind the girl, yipping, "I'm right behind you."

"What?" Crow protested. "Where are you going?"

"Into the cave," Neddy said. She paused at the entrance and gestured for the bird to follow. "Come on."

"But it says — "

"I *know* what it says." Neddy bent and peered into the dark recess. "But I need to find the old man and this is the only place

I've seen that looks like someone – someone who might be human... or close to human – has been here. I think we ought to try it."

"But it's dark in there. I told you I'm not one of those birds that can see in the dark."

"Well, I don't want to ignore it and keep on walking in the desert. Besides, it'll get us out of the sun for a while."

"Come on, Crow," Dog said. "It'll be fun!"

"If it's all the same to you," the bird said, "I'll wait out here."

"What if we come out somewhere else?"

"I'll find you."

Neddy and Crow looked at each other for a moment then, knowing it was settled, the girl and the dog walked into the cave.

It began with an ingress small enough that Neddy had to hunch down to Dog's height to enter. The light from outside narrowed to a sliver as the tunnel curved to one side then the other, and always, gradually, down. Darker and darker until there was no light at all.

She stopped.

Dog bumped into her. "What was that?"

"Me."

"I can't see a thing," Dog said. "Look! Even when I hold my paw right in front of my nose, I can't see it." An edge of panic seeped into his voice. "Am I blind?"

"You're not blind," Neddy said. She could feel her pupils dilating, trying to find even a tiny drop of light. "It's just really dark down here." She shut her eyes. It made no difference, but at least the pupils stopped stretching like a hungry maw.

"Should we go back?" Neddy wondered aloud.

"And have to listen to Crow tell us he *told us so?*" Dog said.

"He didn't *tell us so* about this."

"He'll say he did."

Neddy knew Dog was right.

They felt their way forward a few more steps, Neddy using her hands and Dog using his body to feel along the wall.

Dog thought for a minute before asking, "You're a Galenor, right?"

"Yes….." Neddy blinked, waved her hand in front of her face just in case something had changed (it hadn't), and closed her eyes shut.

"Well," Dog said, "isn't there something you can do?"

"No…." Then Neddy's hand stopped mid-wave. "Wait a minute… of course!" Her hand went to a pocket, felt around, and pulled out a piece of twine. *Let's hope I can remember what*

Rebane said about this. She kneeled on the ground and started sifting through the dirt.

"I can't see anything..." Dog said, blindly tilting his head back and forth. "What are you doing?"

"I'm looking for..." Neddy said more to herself than the dog. She concentrated, letting her fingers search. "Rebane said it should feel like... There! This should do it."

"What?"

"Wait a minute."

Neddy grasped the stone and blindly wrapped it in twine, trusting her hands to do the job without the help of sight. When it felt like it was bundled well enough she knotted the twine, keeping one strand loose. In one hand she held the strand, the stone dangling. With the other hand, she felt along the tunnel's wall, stopping when she found what she needed. A quick whisper to the stone. A few circular whirls of the stone to gain momentum. And... *whack!*

"Yarp!" Dog jumped, startled at the bright spark of light, and tried to shield his eyes with a paw.

Neddy held the twine aloft with the stone swinging at its end like a pendulum. She smiled at her success. It was a good feeling after the past few days. She watched as, starting with a speck of light then crawling across the string wrapped around it, the stone became a softly glowing orb. Neddy's and Dog's eyes slowly adjusted to the light. Ahead of them, the tunnel absorbed the glow for a short distance then turned.

It turned and turned again. Dust floated in the air, kicked up by their trudging feet, drying their throats. More than a few times they stopped for a drink of water.

"How long have we been walking?" Dog asked. It wasn't the first time he'd asked this question.

Now I know how Rebane felt, Neddy thought and she sent a silent apology to the golem.

"My ears are popping," Dog said. "How far down do you think we are?"

Neddy stopped. "Listen," she whispered.

"What?"

"Shush!" The girl closed her eyes and let the sounds come to her. "It's…. I don't know…. *hollow* up ahead."

Feeling a pulse of excitement, Dog trotted ahead, his shadow growing large as it blocked the orb's light. It disappeared around a curve. Neddy heard the padding steps stop, then turn and run back to her.

"Come and look!" Dog bounded toward her.

Neddy wanted to run, but held herself to a trot. She followed the tunnel's bend and felt the change. The air was less cramped, slightly more fresh, and she didn't feel her breath echoing back on her from the walls. One more turn, and she saw it.

They were at the precipice of a cavern. A very large cavern. She thought of yelling something out to see if there was an echo, then decided against it because *I don't know what else might be in here.*

Stalactites hung from above. Stalagmites grew from below. Limestone helictites and lily pads draped the walls. Stone coral sprouted from crevasses. Far below, a rimstone dam held puddles of water that dripped from above and down the walls. Minerals sparkled in the glow of the orb. The ceiling was high, and down below the path widened like a delta pouring into an ocean of rock and dirt.

"Yarp!" Dog barked, nearly sending Neddy out of her skin. *...yarp....* the bark came back to them. "Yep, it's a big room."

"Don't do that!"

"Why not?"

"We might not be alone."

The tunnel opened like a mouth to the vast grotto, and the path continued along the wall, wide enough to be safely walked but narrow enough that Neddy and Dog took careful steps. Shadows danced on the walls as they descended. Neddy swung the orb, watching them wax and wane in the light. But there was one shadow that didn't change. It moved and flickered in its own light.

Dog sniffed the air. "I don't smell anything except us." Dog snorted, then sniffed again. "Wait. No, there *is* something."

"Can you tell what it is?" Neddy had never had to defend herself from a predator, and wondered if she'd need to – or would be able to. *It's okay,* she told herself, *Galenorae aren't prey…. are they?*

"I'm not sure," the dog answered, still sniffing.

Neddy stopped. She listened. "Do you hear something?"

"It sounds… and it smells… like something burning." Dog kept sniffing.

"I think I hear humming," Neddy said. "Do you hear that?"

They continued down the path, but now they were hugging the wall as if it would make them invisible to whatever might be at the end. Dog and Neddy looked at each other then followed where they thought the voice was coming from. When they finally reached the floor of the cavern, they found him tucked into a niche, poking a stick in the flames of a small fire.

"The old man," Neddy whispered.

"Yes's," an old voice floated toward them. "That I am."

Gangly was the word that popped into Neddy's head because that's what the old man was. If a cactus had legs and arms, white hair, a toothy grin and big feet, and if it wore breeches and a loose tunic tied at the waist with a rope and of an unknowable color because of the dirt that covered it, it would look very much like the old man sitting in front of her.

"This here cavern's gots some good acoustics," the man said as they approached. "You's can hear everythin'." He looked at them with surprisingly clear eyes and said, "Did'n ya see my name and the warnin' not to enter o'er the front of the cave?"

"I saw it but I couldn't read it."

"That's odd," the man said, his long fingers scratching his stubbly chin. "It might be's old but it's still's the universal language." He looked at Neddy. "How long's ya been outta the Galenwood?"

"I've lost track of the days."

"Well, that might's explain it."

"This might sound strange," Neddy said, "but are you – by any chance – the old man who dances under the tree when Moon's belly is full?"

"Well," the man said, "I am old. I do like to dance. And I do like to be out in the moonlight, especially when its gotta full belly."

"But do you do them all at once?"

"Mebbee. Sometimes."

Neddy and Dog exchanged looks.

"Ah," Karboney laughed, "I'm jest messin' with ya. I'm the man you's are lookin' for. In fact, I've been waitin' on ya."

"You knew we were coming?" Neddy sat by the fire, realized she hadn't been asked to join, then decided it was alright.

"Of course I knew," the man said. "Haven't you noticed? Moon's not as bright as it should be."

"Yes, I've seen it not go past half-full," Neddy said. "And Sun isn't as bright, either."

"It's because they've lost their heart and breath."

"Can you help me?"

"Us?" Dog added, with a slight wag of the tip of his tail. "We're both going."

Neddy's stomach made a strange sound and she grabbed at her belly. "What was that?"

"You're stomach's growling," Dog said.

"Hmmm…" Karboney said, "are you hungry or somethin'?"

"Yeah. I think I am." Neddy said. "But why? Galenorae don't eat. They *can*. But they don't *need* to."

"You're not in the Galenwood anymore." The old man reached for a piece of bread warming on a rock by the fire. Neddy hadn't seen it before, but as soon as she laid eyes on it her mouth started watering. "Some things change outside the wood," he said as he broke the bread in three and shared it, "some things get forgotten the farther away you get."

"What do you mean?"

"You're hungry. I'll bet you've been thirsty. And…" he eyed the girl, "you've needed to sleep."

"How do you know – "

"And take a look at your knees," he pointed to the scratched skin where tiny specks of blood were drying.

"Galenorae don't bleed," Neddy looked with wonder at her dirty knees. "Look," she said, "my dress is dirty, too." *Wait,* she thought to herself, *should I be worried?* She brushed Dog away before he could get his nose to the knee and lick it clean.

"Annnnd…" Karboney seemed to be enjoying himself, "I'm betting you've already forgotten a couple'a things." He chuckled, then said, "Fer instance, how'd you get downriver?"

Neddy felt just a little unsteady inside. "In a nest….?"

"A nest, you say?"

"Yes."

"You rode downriver in a nest?" Dog said.

"Never mind that," Neddy said. "Why? What's wrong?"

"Did you think of asking for help?" asked the old man.

"Crow helped me."

"Is *that* why he's following you?" Dog asked.

"Never mind that," Neddy said, then, "uuugh… yes."

"Think, girl," Karboney's clear eyes keenly looked into hers.

"I had to go downriver…"

"Did anyone tell you how?"

"Well," Neddy was trying to remember the conversation on the beach, "Beaver told Crow to let me use a nest. But Crow said I needed a boat."

"Why *didn't* you use a boat?"

"I didn't have one."

"Of course you didn't. Why didn't you build one?"

"I don't know how," and again Neddy wondered *is that something Rebane taught me and I didn't listen?*

Karboney pointed to the white twig stuck in Neddy's hair, vainly trying to hold parts of the wild mane in place. "If that thing can be a tree, why can't it be a boat?"

"How did you know – " Neddy reached for the twig. Then she realized *he's right.*

Karboney chewed his bread for a few minutes, swallowed, and said, "No matter. You's here now." He brushed his hands together, knocking crumbs on the ground where a small group of ants were waiting. "We's best get goin'!"

~~~~~~

Karboney led the way, following a trickle of water that ran out of the cavern and into a tunnel. The old man didn't need any light, but Neddy held her orb so she and the dog could see where they were going. It seemed like forever before they emerged into a wide gully where the shadows were growing long.

They scooted their way from the tunnel's mouth in the dirt hill, down to the wash below it, without talking much and only stopping a few times for Dog and Neddy to rest their feet and have a drink. On the third or fourth rest, Crow circled down to them, landing on Dog's back. Neddy shooed the bird off.

"No time to dawdle," the old man told them, "there's still a lots of way to go."

When the desert grew too dark, they stopped. Within the circle of sigils, Neddy and Dog and Crow slept and Karboney waited for them to wake up – a maybe-accidental nudge of an old toe helped with the waking-up part. The next day was a repeat of the day before, and the one after that was a repeat of the day before it.

With each day, there was a little bit less light in the sky until it felt like the world never got past twilight.

They wove from one gully to another. To Neddy, they all looked the same as the last and the next. Only the size of the dry bushes changed, or the numbers of cactus tines that got caught in Dog's hair. Each time they stopped to rest, she would pull as many as she could from the dog's coat. After the first few times she no longer wondered at the stinging and dewlike drops of blood in her fingers. One thing she did notice, though, was the animals. At first, it had just been the three of them but word spread among the creatures that lived in the desert and, little by little – one here, three there – they were being watched. Small birds grasped the branches of bushes and tines of cactuses. Larger birds perched on rocks. Mice and owls came out of their burrows. Tortoises pulled in their legs and stuck their necks out. Snakes and lizards coiled and rested on warm rocks where they could see. Bobcat sat next to Jackrabbit who sat next to Coyote.

"They've never seen a Galenor," Karboney said. "Probably never will again." He looked at the jackrabbit between the two predators. "Some might not even see the end of the day unless they get some sense in their brain." The old man made some clicking sounds. The jackrabbit looked side-to-side, recognized its neighbors, and bolted away.

That night, as they sat in the protective circle, Neddy inspected the bottoms of her feet where the skin was growing thick.

"Them's called callouses," Karboney said. "Grow enough of them and you won't feel the rocks so much no more."

"Will they go away?"

"Is that important to you?"

Neddy wondered whether it was. She decided it wasn't really important but, given the choice, she'd rather the bottoms of her feet were smooth. *How are Erda's so smooth?*, she wondered. She looked to the sky.

"What will we do if Moon's belly doesn't get full?"

"There'll still be a glow comin' from it," Karboney said.

"But… I haven't seen any trees."

"Close your eyes," the old man said. "We'll be there tomorrow."

Chapter Nine: The Tree

"It doesn't look any different than anywhere else." Dog murmured from a corner his mouth.

Neddy agreed but didn't say so out loud.

"Watch it there!" Dog flinched and moved as if to nip at the crow who was perched on Dog's back. "I said you could ride if you picked the cactus and burrs from my coat, *not* if you stabbed me with your beak and talons."

"If you took a bath once in a while," Crow said, spitting out a barbed thorn, "maybe it wouldn't be so easy for the things to get tangled up in your hair. I'll bet some of these have been in here since you were a pup."

"Bathing is overrated," Dog said. "And my hair isn't any messier than the girl's."

"Quaaww…" the bird said, "she's not normal." Crow thought about how that sounded and added, "In a very nice way."

"Hush, you two," Neddy said. "You've been going on all day. It's very tiring."

Dog gave Crow one last shake. The bird grabbed a clump of hair to hang on and regained his balance on the dog's back.

They were on a wide plateau carpeted with black rocks, smooth and round like the stones at the bottom of the river. The three waited and watched as the old man, bent over so his nose nearly touched the ground, surveyed and studied each rock, occasionally picking one up and turning it in his hand then carefully putting it back where it had been. He mumbled to himself, or maybe not to himself, as he searched.

Crow cocked his head to one side. "What's he looking for?"

Neddy shook her head and brushed a frizzed curl from her face.

"Maybe the tree is very, very tiny," Dog said. "Small enough to fit under a rock."

"That's ridiculous," Crow said.

"Why?" Dog said.

"Quaaawww – " Crow started.

"Found it!" Karboney cackled. "Hoo-hoo-hooooo! I knew it was around here somewhere."

"What?" Neddy strained to see, not sure if she should go to the old man after he'd admonished them to stay put until he told them to move.

"The perfect spot," Karboney said. "Why're you all just standing there? Come on over here." He gestured with one hand for them to join him. In the palm of his other hand he held a stone. "Girl," he said, "come take a look at this." He waited for Neddy to get close enough then said, "You see's how it's different?"

"Ummm…. no?"

"Eck, girl… you haven't been away from home *that* long." Karboney grabbed Neddy's hand and pressed the stone into her palm. "Look at it. Real close."

It was a small stone. She could easily fit five of the same size in her fist. Scorched black on top from days under Sun's heat and light. White on the bottom, and slight red ridge circling it like a belt holding the black and white together.

"Closer," Karboney said.

"What?" Dog wagged his tail. "Lemme see."

"Quaw!" Crow grasped hair in his talons. "Hold still."

Neddy rubbed the rock between her fingers and thumb. It felt warm and tingly. And it pulsed, as if there was a heart beating deep inside. She opened her hand, letting the stone rest on her flat, upturned palm. The pulsations slowed and stopped. But, just barely, she could still feel the tingle resonating from its center.

"What is it?" Neddy asked.

"It's da stone that will help da tree grow," Karboney said. "Now, holds on to it for a bit whilst I…" his sentence drifted off as he dug in a pouch on his hip.

With the tips of his fingers he pulled out a small bunch of seeds and dropped them in the palm of his hand. Sifting through them with a long finger, he separated the seeds, studying each one until, "Ah… this one." he held a wrinkled, odd-shaped seed the color of old muck.

"Here, hold this for me," he said, giving the seed to Neddy. He dropped the other seeds back into the pouch.

"What's this?"

"Our tree."

"I take it back, Dog," Crow said with more than a hint of sarcasm. "Tiny trees under rocks isn't ridiculous at all."

Karboney eyed the bird. "Don't listen to that," he said to the dog. "I've seen tiny trees under rocks. Giant trees in the clouds.

Even trees that can swim and fly…. *But*," he pointed at the wrinkled seed in Neddy's hand, "they all come from seeds." He looked to the sky. "Sun is close to the horizon and Moon will be risin' soon. We need to hurry."

Kneeling on the ground, Karboney poked his finger in the spot where the stone that was now in Neddy's hand had been. "That seed is the tree that holds what you're looking for," he said as he dug a small hole, and dribbled a considerable amount of spit into it.

When he'd moistened the dirt in the hole to some satisfaction, he took the seed from Neddy and buried it. Then he took the stone and placed it on top of the tiny mound of dirt over the seed. Standing up, he dusted the dirt from his hands and, keeping his eyes on the stone, he took several steps backwards, then proclaimed, "Here!"

The girl, the dog and the bird had no idea what to do or if they should say anything. So they stood still, looking between the stone and the old man.

"Eck!" Karboney grunted. "Comes over here," he gestured, waving both hands back and forth in a come-along motion. "We needs to get into a protective circle."

"Why?" Crow asked.

"Heh-heh… you'll see."

Neddy looked at the sheet of stones across the ground. There was no dirt for her to draw a sigil in. She thought for a moment then reached into a pocket that produced a small chunk of chalk. Apologizing to the dark stones on the desert bloor for marking them, and promising that the chalk would disappear in the wind and next rain, she drew symbols on the rocks, making a circle around her, Karboney, the dog and the bird.

"Now," Karboney said, "makes a second circle around thems two." He pointed at Dog and Crow.

"Why?" Crow asked.

"You'll see."

Neddy repeated the steps, encircling the bird and dog with sigils, whispering as she went. When she was done, Karboney sat cross-legged outside the smaller circle but within the larger one. She sat next to him.

Shadows grew long and Sun, finished with its work for the day, stepped behind the horizon.

"What now?" Dog asked.

"We wait."

They took this time to rest, lying back on the hard ground, trying to ignore the stones that stuck up into their backs.

Neddy gazed upward, knowing the stars were on their way, but hoping they were still far enough that she had time to finish.

Finish what? She tried to imagine what she would have to do before returning to Galenwood, but had no idea what was coming next, or after that, or after that.

"If it wasn't for the stars," Crow said, holding up one wing in front of his face, "I wouldn't be able to see my feathers."

"Moon's lost its breath," Karboney said. "It's gettin' harder to climb into the sky. But give it time."

Crow saw Dog had fallen asleep and tucked himself into the dog's coat. The dog dream-twitched his feet but continued to snore, unaware of the bird. Neddy watched the two, glad to see them becoming friends – of some sort.

~~~~~~

Moon peeked over the dark horizon, washing the desert with a pale wave of light that creeped along the ground towards the mountains across the sky. The light touched the stone atop the buried seed, and the stone began to glow. Red, black and white swirled, slowly at first then gaining speed, awakened by the moon. Swirling faster, glowing brighter with a kind of cool warmth, the stone began to shake, then bounce and then –

"Heh! Here we go," Karboney said. "Now, no matter what happens, don't step out of your circle. Not until I tell you to."

A grin stretched across his thin, wizened face as he watched the ground where the seed was buried.

Dog yawned and rolled over on top of the bird.

"Quaw!" Crow squeezed out from under the dog. "Watch where you're going."

Dog smacked his lips and thought a biscuit might be nice. Then he looked at the glowing stone bouncing up and down, and *wuffed.*

Moon was now wholly into the sky above the horizon, its weakened belly less than half full. But, even with the feeble light, the stone jumped twice as high as before and, landing on the mound, pummeled itself down into the ground. Burrowing down to the seed. And when the seed and stone touched, the ground shuddered, rumbled, rolled and heaved a belch from the hole made by the stone. There was a pause for a moment and then a long tendril as thick as Neddy's arm shot straight into the air.

"Ayip!" Dog jumped back. Crow reached for the scraggly tail and kept it from leaving their circle.

"Oh!" Neddy groaned, covering her nose. "What's that smell?"

"That's the tree," Karboney said. The grin hadn't left his face. "This be the tree of the Gloks. They's gots the breath and the heart, so we gots to go into a Glok tree to get them back."

Neddy watched the malodorous tendril worm its way upward, out of the ground.

"Is this the part where you start dancing?" Crow squawked.

"No time for that. Too much to git done."

The tendril grew thick and tall, splitting at the top into arms of branches, each splitting into smaller branches, growing foul-smelling leaves along the way. The main tendril, now a thick trunk, and everything that grew from it was same color as the seed from which it sprouted: muck. Dark brown, black and putrid green. Where most trees had bark it had goo that roiled around, up, down, in and out of the trunk and branches. It stank. Everything about it smelled rotten. The odor enveloped the tree like an unseen fog, and with the trunk it expanded out and out, to the edge of the protective circle of sigils.

Neddy, not wanting to find out what might happen if the circle was broken, whispered words of strength to the sigils.

Pressing against the sigiled enclosure, moving around the circle and slithering across the invisible dome of protection above Karboney, Neddy and the two petrified animals. Unable to penetrate the protection brought by the sigils, the tree yanked itself away, leaving behind thick and slimy mud that slid down the sides of the dome.

Finally, the trunk pulled itself into a form that looked like a willow tree, if willow trees were made of muck and dripped muck from mucky leaves.

Karboney pointed. "There," he said, "you see that hole?"

Neddy saw a spot in the tree where it was darker than the putrid darkness around it. "That's a hole?"

"That's where we're going in."

"*What?*"

"You wants the breath and the heart? That's where you gotsta go to get 'em."

Neddy stared at the dripping, gooey sludge that was the tree. She turned to the old man. "I can't go in there."

"Then you fail your Quest," Karboney said. "Can't no amount of heroes help you then. Go home and explains it to the golem, and try to enjoy yer last days." He looked at her. "You *can* do this."

Neddy groaned and stared at the hole some more. "Okay," she finally said, "what do I need to do?"

"You go down an *get 'em!*"

"What about us?" Dog asked.

"You two stays here with me," Karboney said. "Stays in yer circle."

"I can do that," Crow said.

"I can't come and help?" Dog said.

"No. This hasta be just the girl."

"We'll be right here." Crow ruffled and preened his feathers hoping he looked as calm and collected as he absolutely was not feeling.

"You're gonna see Gloks down there," Karboney said. "Yous'll know dem because, what with the Dark makin' them from what's dredged from the pits of rot, they'll look and smell like the tree. They's gonna stink somthin' real bad." He paused to give Neddy a moment to absorb, then said, "There's one rule you need to know. It's a big one, and if you don't keep to it you'll lose what you're after." The old man faced Neddy, looking at the girl to be sure she was listening. "Once you go into that hole you can'ts make a sound. Don't speaks at all. Don't talks to nuthin'. Don'ts talk to yourself. Don't even makes a grunt. Nothin' at all until you're back out, and even then you's gotsta wait until I say so."

"But, what if – "

"No." Karboney held up a spindly finger. "That's the one rule you must not break. No buts or whats or anything else."

Neddy took a deep breath, letting it out slowly as Rebane had taught her to do. She pulled the water and biscuit pouches from their pockets, took a long drink, then poured some into the bowl-cap and set it and the opened pouch of biscuits inside the inner circle. She wished she'd eaten a few, but now there wasn't time.

"Ready?" Karboney asked.

Neddy nodded but had to force herself to answer. "Yes." She reached down to move a stone and break the ring.

"One more thing," Karboney said.

Neddy froze. "What?"

"This tree's only here as long as Moon is in the sky. When Moon's gone, the tree's gone."

"And what happens if I'm still inside."

"Well...."

"*What?*" Neddy looked up to the moon. "It's already high up!"

"Yep," Karboney said, "You's best git a move on."

Neddy rolled her eyes and started to move her foot to kick a sigiled rock aside. Then she remembered *it's not their fault* and she stopped. She bent and whispered thanks to the stones, and gently moved them apart wide enough for her to step out of their protection.

She wiped a loose clump of dirt from her dress. "Okay. Here I go."

~~~~~~

Neddy didn't think it was possible, but the stench was worse inside the trunk than outside. She tried holding her breath, but that just meant her lungs were filled with an odor so putrid it felt like a thick ball of muck instead of air. Compared to what she was breathing now, Dog smelled like the fruit of bliss. First she told herself *this won't take long.* Then she told herself *I'll get used to it after a while.* After that she told herself *it's permeating my skin and very being and I will smell this way forever.* She didn't say anything, though. Didn't complain. Didn't grumble. Didn't moan even a tiny bit. Because she remembered the rule: no talking.

Gingerly, she carefully stepped on coarse and irregular bundles of fibrous root, her hands clutching at thin and scraggling roots that hung down from the dirt around her. She gripped with her toes and fingers, steadying herself against the mucky, stinking, slime that covered everything. She held her lips tightly closed and didn't look up. If even the smallest drop of sludge fell into her mouth or nose… she forced herself not to think about it.

The rooted shaft under the tree went so far down Neddy couldn't see where it ended. Down the center of it all, the taproot spiraled in the musty light. Neddy, trying to distract herself, thought about Rebane's lessons on gasses. She wondered how large the fireball would be if someone lit a flame. Her foot slipped on a glob of something, making her catch her breath. The insides of her body fought back and, silently, she gagged and stopped thinking about anything outside this realm of rancid, putrid, fetid, rank that she previously could not have imagined was existable.

At first all she could hear was the sucking sounds each time she lifted a foot out of the muck to take a step forward. Then, faintly at first but, bit by bit, growing louder, sounds wafted up from the depths. Grunting and growling and something that might have been a language.

Finally, the taproot ended, its tip dangling to the floor of the hollowed-out chamber where Gloks shuffled about. None were taller than Neddy, and they resembled humans in that they had round bodies, legs, arms and a head. Other than that, they looked like what you might see if you took a handful of sludge from the bottom of a bog and splatted it with more of the same sludge. They milled around, bumping into each other, falling over, blubbering arguments over whose fault it was. At first Neddy thought they were just plodding around, but then she saw the holes burrowed into the wall. Each hole just tall and wide enough for a Glok to pass through, which they were all trying to do, in and out, all at the same time. In a roundabout kind of circle, punctuated with the bumping and falling and arguing, each Glok would take a rough burlap bag from a large pile of the sacks in the middle of the room and go into a burrow. The ones coming out from the burrows were empty-handed,

She stepped off the root and moved towards one side of the room. Whereas the tree and it's parts were mucky and Glok-like, the floor and walls around it were as clean as any soil in a garden or field. Neddy let herself lean into the earthen wall, her toes digging into the dirt, feeling its connection with the world, soaking in the strength and the wonderful cleanliness of it.

Neddy tiptoed towards the pile of bags, moving silently around the Gloks. *Which one do I take? Karboney didn't say anything about burlap sacks.* She reached for one, reconsidered, reached for another, and reconsidered again. She realized that, not only were they all the same, even if they were different she had no way of knowing which one to choose. She closed her eyes grabbed the first bag her fingers touched, slipped her arm through the loop of drawstring's twine, and shrugged the bag onto her shoulder.

Making her way back along the wall and onto the taproot, Neddy wasn't sure whether it had been harder to keep from slipping on her way down or pulling herself up. The muscles in her legs burned with fatigue and her hands were raw where fibers had cut into her skin as she grabbed the tendrils of roots for balance. She wanted to rest, and she felt anger towards the old man creeping into her chest. *He should be doing this,* she thought. *He certainly isn't like the rest of us. I'm pretty sure Dog said there wasn't any smell about him. He just pops up in the middle of the desert and knows exactly where we're from and what we're doing—*

Distracted by her thoughts, Neddy didn't look well enough at the root she was reaching for and it snapped when she pulled on it. Down she went, "oomph," onto her belly, sliding down more than twice her own length before she was able to stop herself by digging her fingers into the fiber of the root. *Why do I have to do this? Why can't someone help me?* Putrid slop covered her face and she spat, trying in vain to get the taste out of her mouth. She gagged. She couldn't hold it back. With a wrenching heave she vomited, ejecting bile and muck that fell down to the chamber below.

She froze.

The arguing and cursing continued. The Gloks hadn't noticed.

With a silent sigh of relief, Neddy pulled herself upright and continued the climb until she reached the top and slipped out of the trunk.

Neddy breathed in deep, filling her lungs with fresh air. She waved to Dog and Crow, and started to say something to them but was stopped by the old man's hand that covered her mouth and held it there.

"Don't talk!" Karboney hissed. He didn't pull his hand away until Neddy nodded that she understood. "Now," he said, "this is what ya do. First, pull that bag off 'f yer shoulder and set it on the ground. Right there." He waited for the girl to follow his instructions. "Okay.... now ya gotsta listen real close." He waited again for Neddy to nod. "This is what's ya do," he repeated himself. "You's think – think really hard – puts a picture in yer head of what it is that you wants. Picture the heart of the Mountain and the breath of the Water. Now—" he interrupted himself, "—I know, I know.... You've never seen them. Just picture what you think they might look like. What do they feel like? Think of Moon and Sun."

Neddy imagined waves rushing and splashing, catching and holding the air in bubbles and bringing them down beneath the water's surface. She imagined the depths of a mountain where the molten rocks beat with the pulse of a massive heart. When she was ready, she looked to Karboney.

"Now," he grinned, "open the bag."

Neddy pulled the twine and opened the bag. She looked inside.

"You can talk now," Karboney said.

Sticking her hand into the sack, she felt around. She held the bag upside down and shook it.

"It's empty."

"What?" Karboney grabbed the bag. "It can't be." He repeated Neddy's search stuffing his hand inside and wriggling his fingers, and shaking it upside-down. "Did you picture the heart? And the breath?"

"Yes."

Karboney sat on the ground, baffled. He thought for a bit, then looked up at the girl. "By any chance, didjya says somethin' while you's was down there?"

"No!" Neddy was already tired and frustrated, and now she was starting to feel angry. How could he accuse her of that? How— *uh-oh*....

"I see's it on yer face," the old man stood up. "Tell me."

"I didn't *say* anything." Neddy could barely find the breath to speak. "I *didn't*."

"What?"

"When I slipped. When I fell. I—"

"You what?"

"I went *oomph*," she said, emphasizing the *oomph*.

"Ack!"

"And then I threw up."

"Ack and argh!" The old man, arms flailing above his head, tramped in a circle.

"But I didn't *say* anything!" Neddy protested.

"It's not just yer voice. Not just yer words. It's any sound ya makes." Karboney started to scold but when he saw the girl's face he couldn't. She was already punishing herself enough. "Oh, young-un.... what were you thinking?"

"I don't know!" Neddy cried, "I was wishing I had some help. I can't do this."

She threw the sack on the ground, and threw herself next to it.

"I've failed, haven't I?"

"Well...."

"I *have*. And now.... now..."

"Quaaaawww.... we're doomed."

Dog thumped the bird with a paw and, ignoring Karboney's earlier admonishments to stay within the circle, went to the girl and nuzzled up against her."

"I'm so sorry," Neddy said as she hugged the dog for comfort. She'd never cried before, but she knew what tears were and could feel them welling up in her eyes.

"Hold on just a bit there…" Karboney said, putting a hand on the girl's shoulder. "It's not all that bad."

"Yes it is. I failed. I didn't get the breath or the heart. And now the world is going to end."

"Well," Crow said, still sitting in the smaller circle. "It won't really end. It'll just be ruled by Dark, that's all."

"You're not helping," Dog barked at the bird.

"No, no, no…" Karboney said. "Look up. At the moon." He pointed and Neddy looked. "You see? Moon is only barely past halfways across the sky."

Neddy looked. A tear trickled down her cheek.

"There's still time," the old man said.

"Time for what?" Neddy wiped the tear on her arm and buried her face into Dog's coat, relishing the smell over what she'd been breathing below.

"This tree is here until Moon sets. There's time to go back. Git another bag."

"I can do that?"

"Sure… of course you can." Karboney wasn't entirely sure, but it sounded right. "Just make sure ya do it quick and you's get right back out. Gotta be out before Moon sets."

"I can do that!"

Neddy jumped up, ran to the tree, and dove into the hole.

"Wait," Karboney said, too late, "I'll go with you…" He watched the girl slip into the trunk.

"Quaaaaw…" Crow stretched his neck forward, his eyes widened.

"She knows what to do," Dog said, "right?"

"Yes," Karboney said, "she does." This time he believed what he said. He reached for the burlap bag lying on the ground and picked it up. "This could make for a good pouch," he said, turning it over in his hands.

"Could you please stop doing that?" A voice came from inside the bag.

Karboney stopped. He looked at Dog. Dog looked at the old man, ears perked. Crow took one hop backwards, shifting his attention towards the bag.

"You've already ruined my web. And now you're going to *crush me.*"

The old man set the bag down. Dog *wuffed* and sniffed at it.

A very small leg, fuzzy with brown and orange hairs, reached out over the edge of the bag's mouth, curling as it bent in segments, grasping the burlap with tiny claws. Then another, and another. A pair of hairy feelers tapped the outside of the bag and the spider pulled herself out. Hairy pedipalps wiggled on either side of a pair of fangs beneath four pairs of eyes. The body and abdomen were the same colors as the legs, and just as fuzzy.

No bigger than the old man's thumbnail, the spider hunkered down, gathered herself and sprung straight up to land on Dog's forehead. The dog's eyes crossed themselves trying to see her.

The little jumping spider sat back on her hindlegs and waved her forelegs in the air, shouting angrily, "What in the name of all websilks is going on?" It was surprising how loud such a small creature could be.

Chapter Ten: The Tree Again

For the first time since her first day Neddy's hair wasn't a wild frizz of red mess. Because now it was plastered against her head, thick with the muck that dripped off the roots under the tree. She'd climbed down the taproot quickly, sliding more than stepping. When she reached the floor beneath, she wanted to stick her nose in the dirt wall just to breath it's scent. *No time to waste*, she told herself, resisting such a reprieve from the stench. Hugging her back against the earthen side of the chamber, she ambled sideways then crawled across the dirt floor to the pile of burlap bags. Holding one arm out with fingers waggling, she grabbed the first one they touched, then scooted backwards across the floor and along the wall to the taproot. All the while, she pursed her lips to keep any sound, anything at all, from coming out. Bag slung over her shoulder, she reached the root and started climbing back up.

She was several paces upward when she heard the shuffling stop. A moment later something that sounded like a phlegm-soaked voice cried out.

Neddy froze and looked down to see one Glok holding up a fist. It was pointing at her and it made the sound again. The eyes of every Glok in the room followed the pointing fist to where the girl was balancing on the slimy root.

~~~~~~

All around the trunk of the Glok tree the ground rolled and waved in jolts, but the protective sigils held strong.

From deep inside the mucky tree, a sound gurgitated like the *mwaaw* of a hundred angry cats, the croaks of a thousand indignant frogs, the burbled flatulence of the thickest bog, wailing out through the hole in the tree's trunk like a distressed banshee. A gust of hot, putrid wind blew out from deep inside the tree.

Dog jumped and barked, laying his ears back flat and baring his teeth.

Karboney sat, cross-legged and eyes closed, his thin hands touching the ground for balance, quietly whispering.

Crow stared. Immobilized.

The spider crawled back into her burlap bag.

All four stayed inside the inner circle of sigils and runes.

~~~~~~

Neddy dug deep for every bit of strength she had and reached for one root after another, climbing as fast as she could. She didn't want to look down. She didn't have to. She could feel the Gloks below her, clambering over each other, grunting and spitting, to get to the thick root and up to her.

The thick main root shook and *whump!* snapped like a whip. Gloks flew in all directions and Neddy, losing her grip, slid down losing half the distance she'd covered. Not hesitating, she bit her tongue and grabbed the nearest piece of fiber hanging from above and pulled herself up. Hand-over-hand, she climbed, remembering the skills she'd learned among the vines in the Galenwood.

Another *whump!* But this time Neddy hung on, dug her fingers in, and kept going up. Then she realized... *it's not just whumping.... It's shrinking!* Starting in the chamber, everything was crushing inward. Rolling up and squeezing itself closed like a tube of slop. Most of the Gloks disappeared, subsumed into the walls of the chamber as rocks and dirt crashed together, but a few of them slurred into the sludge being squeezed up. Neddy grabbed at the underground limbs and branches of root as fast as she could, the force of the tree closing in on itself building pressure beneath her, pushing her up. She felt a Glok touching for her feet. Then another grabbing her leg.

Scrambling as fast as her legs and arms could climb Neddy thought she sensed something from above. A shift in the air. Something that sounded like the words she whispered when she spoke the to the runes and sigils. She kept reaching, but now her body was being pushed up faster than she could grab the roots the force building beneath her was so strong. She closed her eyes and held her breath. And she tried to quiet her mind except for the thought of being outside... out of the stinking, soggy-mucked tree.

~~~~~~

"Aiyip! Aiyip!" Dog kept barking at the sounds and whatever else was coming from the hole.

"The tree!" Crow jumped up and down, pointing with feathers on both wings, squawking in panic. "The tree is shrinking!"

The spider wondered what was going on but stayed deep inside the bag.

Karboney, seemingly oblivious to everything going on around them, kept his eyes shut and didn't stop whispering.

And then everything stopped. The air. The noise. The dripping muck. As if the world was taking one last breath before –

A *CRACK!* shattered the air and the tree sucked itself inward with a *whoosh!* A cacophony of groans, oozings and splats filled the vacuum it left behind. Every branch, twig and gooey leaf shrunk down, zipping into the ground. Every root and tendril sucked upward to the surface of the earth and, just before squeezing shut, as if hocking the biggest loogie of phlegm ever seen, the tree spat Neddy out, followed by a thick, flying puddle of Gloks.

Hissing like a squealing tea kettle, the tree wriggled and squiggled and shrunk until it was once again the wrinkled seed.

The ejected Gloks spluttered around in circles, bumping into each other, then ran away.

Neddy sat. Eyes still closed, lips still pursed. Breathing through her nose so she couldn't squeak even the smallest of sounds. She wiped at her eyes with the skirt of her dress, but it was just as mucked up as everything else. So she blinked through the tiny globules dripping from her eyelashes and held up the burlap bag triumphantly.

Karboney jumped up and out of the circle, dancing a jig so hard he was almost wriggling out of his skin. He squealed, "Think of what you want! Come on, now. The breath of the Water. The heart of the Mountain. Picture 'em."

Neddy rolled her shoulders back and stretched her neck, the way Rebane had taught her when she needed to calm herself. She took deep breaths…. one…. two… three…. She imagined the breath. She imagined the heart. And when she was ready… She opened the bag.

Chapter Eleven: The Quest Continues

Neddy dipped underwater again, letting the river's current pull the dried muck from her hair and skin and dress. Dog swam in circles, then climbed out and stood on some grass growing nearby. He shook his entire body, nose to tail-tip, hard enough for the water to spray Crow who perched in a tree just above.

"Watch it!" Crow squawked.

Dog smiled and shook some more.

"I really wish he'd come with us," Neddy said, walking out of the water and sitting next to Dog. She watched the spider wrap something in silk and carry it into the burlap bag where she had made her home. "I'm going to miss the old man."

~~~~~~

After the tree had shrunk back to a seed, they'd waited until the desert was awash with Sun's morning light before they began walking again. Karboney stayed with them the rest of the way across the desert, to where the river, having wound itself around a valley, was in front of them again and rolling towards the range of mountains. "Follows that there river," the old man had said. "It'll take you's to the feets of the mountains."

"You're not coming with us?"

"Naw. It's yer Quest, not mine."

"What do we do when we get to the mountains?"

"Ya sees that big lump?" He raised a skinny arm and pointed with a boney finger towards the mountains. "Right there between them two peaks."

For the past few days, Neddy *had* noticed a mound growing between the two highest peaks. She didn't think it had been there before but hadn't asked about it, thinking – telling herself – it must just be her mind remembering wrong. Other things had been odd. Things that didn't happen back in the Galenwood. Now, she got hungry. And thirsty. She found herself growing tired, her feet hurting, and wanting to sleep. Her dress, always clean white, was dirty and stained. For a mound in the mountain range to be unfamiliar was probably just another odd thing. But now that Karboney was pointing it out, she thought that maybe it wasn't just fuzzy memory.

"Is that new?"

"Of course it's new." Karboney looked at her. "That range," he jutted a chin towards the far range, "it ain'tn't what it's s'posed to be."

It took a bit for the old man's words to unwriggle themselves in her brain for her to understand what he'd said.

"So, the next part of my Quest is to get to that big, new, mound."

"Yup."

She gazed across at the new outline on the horizon, "How does a mountain just show up like that?"

"I reckon someone's buildin' it."

"How do you build a mountain?"

"Ya uses whatever materials ya gots," Karboney shrugged. "Not sure. Never done it myself."

"Do you know who might be doing it?"

"Oh, I am *sure* of that. It's the Gloks." He crossed his arms and added, "I'm'a callin' it the Gloky Mountain."

"Gloky Mountain…. But what materials would they have?"

Karboney answered with a snort and a chuckle.

"Oh…"

"Yup."

"And I have to go there?"

"Yup."

"You know that's not funny. In fact, it's pretty disgusting."

"Yup." He smacked his lips with the last letter of the word, making a popping sound.

The two looked at the mountains for a bit longer, neither of them really wanting to go their separate ways.

"Are you sure you can't come with us?"

"No," the old man turned to the girl, "I can't. Ya gotsta do it yerself."

"What do I do when I get to… Gloky Mountain?" A groan creaked into her voice when she said the name.

"Can't tell ya that," Karboney had said. "What I can tell ya, and which you's already knows, is that pretty soon Moon and Sun are gonna be lookin' at each others straight across the horizons, both risin' and settin' at the same time. That's when the stars is gonna line up. You's best be done and finished by then. Or – "

"I know. Or Dark will rule the world."

With a nod, the old man turned and started on his way, but he stopped and turned back.

"That little spider…" he said. "You says you'd wished for some help when you's was down in the roots."

"Yes?"

He scratched his chin. "It's possible," he said, "she weren't in that sack by accident."

He nodded again, and turned, and this time he went on his way and didn't turn back.

~~~~~~

Neddy didn't need to shade her eyes to look across the river. The day was new, but the sky was dim. Sun was growing weaker. Neddy was concerned, but she didn't share her worry with the others. "It shouldn't be too hard to walk along its edge. Looks like there's grass on both sides all the way down."

"Why don't you build a boat?" Crow squawked.

Neddy ignored the bird. She was getting better at doing that. She thought of asking the river and grasses for advice, but she didn't want to go through that frustration again. And she felt confident that she could find her way without their help. It felt good. A little bit scary, but mostly good. It was the second time she'd been led to the river and left to go on her own, and this time she felt okay about it. *Besides*, she told herself, *if we get lost I can always ask them then, and they can point us in the right direction, can't they?* She wasn't sure of the answer to that, but decided to tell herself it was *yes, they could.*

Dog, having shaken most of the water from his coat, trotted over to her. "Which side do we walk on?"

"I don't think it matters," Neddy said. She reached for Spider's burlap bag and slung it over her shoulder. Spider hopped out to see where they were going.

The other bag, the one with the breath and the heart, was safely tucked into a pocket in the skirt of her frock. She'd put it there after showing everyone the contents, and she wasn't going to take it out again until — she wasn't sure about that part, but knew she'd know when the time was right.

They started walking, Spider on Neddy's shoulder and Crow on Dog's back.

"The old man said something about heroes," Dog shook just enough to dislodge the bird's talons which had gone a bit too deep. "What's he talking about?"

"Every Galenor finds a hero during their Quest. The heroes he was talking about helped all the Galenorae before me." Neddy looked upward.

Dog thought about this, but Crow said, "You're going to have to tell us more than that."

Neddy thought for a moment. *How would Rebane tell it?* "After Water and Mountain won the war against Dark they made our world, Galen, and everything on land and in water."

"They made us?" Dog didn't look up, but the one ear that could stand up was raised.

"A long time ago they made your ancestors," said Neddy.

"And they made the Gloks," Crow added.

"Dark made the Gloks."

"But the heroes," said Dog. "Who made them?"

"They weren't made as heroes. That's what they became."

"Quaaaw... what does that mean?"

"She'd probably tell you if you two would stop interrupting," chirped the spider on the girl's shoulder.

The bird and the dog went quiet and Neddy told them about the heroes. She tried to tell it as Rebane had told her.

"First there were the Galenorae: Girl, Woman, and Crone. Crone was the wisest, with all the knowledge from everything made by Water and Mountain. Plants and animals, stones and rocks. Air and fire. Woman knew the plants and animals, but in a different way than Crone. Woman was their protector. She watched over them and kept them safe. Girl was young and learning, and she had the innocence and wonder of a child. The three Galenorae lived in the Galenwood where its people are protected from the world outside. At first Woman and Crone were the Girl's teachers, but soon they realized they couldn't do that and still fulfill their other responsibilities.

"Crone spoke to the rocks, asking for one of their strongest to help guide Girl. Obsidian stepped forward and offered its services. Then Woman went to the animals and asked if there was someone with patience who would be willing to teach the girl. A tortoise named Gilananna stepped forward. Crone and Woman and Girl, Obsidian and Tortoise, went to the top of the Great Galen Tower, the highest place in the Galenwood. There, the Galenorae called to Mountain and Water, asking for their help. Mountain and Water answered, and Obsidian and Tortoise became one. They transformed into a golem and were called Golem Gilananna. After that, every time there's an Ascension, Obsidian bonds with a new hero and the old hero goes to live with Crone. Then, at the next Ascension, it becomes a star and joins the rest of the stars in the sky."

"How many heroes are there?" asked Spider.

"As many as there are stars in the sky."

"So, your Quest is to find your hero, for the Ascension...."

Dog was trying to understand. "What's an Ascension?"

145

"It's when – "

"Quaw!" Crow flapped his wings and gripped the dog's hair. "What was that?"

Dog stopped and sniffed the air and nearly gagged.

Neddy smelled it, too. From the corner of her eye she saw something move.

"It just ran across behind us," Crow, still grasping dog's coat, turned his head backwards and sideways, trying to see the movement again. "It looked like a shadow."

"Everything looks like a shadow," said Dog, "there's hardly any light from the sun."

Crow squawked. "It looked like – "

"Dark like muck?" Neddy couldn't fix her sight on it, but she could definitely smell it.

"A Glok?" Dog's ear stood up and a low growl rumbled from deep inside his throat.

"What's a Glok?" Spider had been inside her burlap bag when Neddy went into the tree and had missed all the excitement.

They told her about the Gloks. What had made them. Where they came from. What they were made of.

"So *that's* what that's been," said Spider. "I've been smelling it since before the old man left."

"Why didn't you say anything?"

Spider shrugged the shoulders of her four front legs. "I thought it was the dog."

"Hey, I'm not *that* bad."

"Says you."

"Makes me glad I don't have a sense of smell," Crow chimed in.

"You can walk if you like," the offended dog shook his body, knocking the bird to the ground.

"Will you guys please stop?" Neddy stomped a foot and waved her hands at the three. "We have a Glok following us."

"More than one," the spider sat back on her four hind legs. "A whole lot more."

It was quiet while everyone looked around them, searching for something they knew was there but they could not see.

"Do you think," Crow gurgled, "that maybe we should get going?"

"And go faster?" Dog added.

Crow hopped back on Dog's back and they all resumed walking with greater purpose than before.

The light grew even more dim and Neddy knew that soon it would be gone. She also knew they couldn't count on Moon to guide them with its light. It was as weak as Sun.

The dark shapes followed behind them. Neddy and Dog walked faster, but the shapes not only kept pace but spread out so they were on either side, as well as behind them. The thickening rank smell told them the Gloks were closing the distance.

"We should run," Neddy said.

Dog didn't need to be told twice and ran with the bird clinging to his back. Bounding in leaps across the grass along the river's side, surprising himself at how fast he could go. Before this the worst that had chased the dog was a shopkeeper shooing him from the garbage bin. Never had he felt his life in danger as it was now. Never before had the dog known that if he slowed down, even just a little bit... Fear kept the legs going. Fear and the sharp talons digging through the coat and into his back.

Spider managed to crawl into the dark safety of the burlap bag while Neddy ran as fast as the dog, wishing the grass would part and make a path like she'd seen it do in the Galenwood. But these were not Galenwood grasses. So she ran, feeling the rocks and dry sticks and burrs. Anything that was small and sharp seemed to be lining up beneath her feet.

The sun was gone now, resting behind a horizon that could barely be seen in the weak glow of the meager sunset. It was going to be very dark very soon.

Crow squawked, "Do you still have the orb?"

Neddy panted, "I'd have to make a new one."

And then they heard it. The sound of a waterfall, rushing and crashing ahead of them. Which meant that, also ahead of them, would be the cliff from where the water was falling.

Neddy tried to think.

"What do we do?" Dog gasped the words out between heaving gulps for air.

"I don't know!"

Around them, closer and closer, the dark shadows came. *They're pushing us towards the cliff*, thought Neddy. It was getting harder not to panic, but she could see it getting darker ahead of them. *They're surrounding us!* She looked from side to side, searching for an escape.

It was so dark now, if it wasn't for the sound of rushing water Neddy wouldn't have been able to tell which direction she was going.

"Quawk! I can't see anything."

The crashing water grew louder.

"We have to stop," said Neddy, "or we might run off the cliff." She slowed down, listening for the dog's breathing and only stopping when she could feel the animal beside her.

"What's that?" Spider emerged from her sack, sensing the air.

Unable to see, Dog sniffed the air. "All I can smell is Glok." More sniffing.

"Shh!" said Neddy, and she pointed even though nobody could see. "Look."

It didn't seem possible, but the blackness in front of them grew darker. Thicker and heavier. Taller it grew, rising high into the air like a black wave reaching for the highest crest.

Neddy fell to the ground, wrapping her arms around the dog. Dog shoved his nose under her arm and the bird tried to squeeze in between them. Spider burrowed herself into Neddy's tangled hair. They all shut their eyes, bracing themselves. Frightened beyond words, finding strength in each other. Waiting for the engulfing crash to come down on them, horrified beyond imagination of what would happen after that. They held their breath.

But the wave didn't crash down upon them. Neddy looked up just in time to see it rise from the ground, and spring over them into the horde of Gloks. She watched it changing shape, growing massive arms to stretch out and grab the stinking blobs, rising with what looked like the head of a stag with hundred-pointed antlers, then a great wolf, a badger, a raven – the head of one rising and striking and plunging, then rising again as another. Gloks scattered in every direction, colliding and grunting spluttered curses at each other, shrieking as they were hoisted into the air and flung far, far away.

When the last Glok was gone, the shadowy thing that had saved them looked at the group huddled together on the ground, then looked to the sky and misted away into nothing.

Chapter Twelve: The Waterfall

They'd slept as much as they could, which wasn't a lot. Moon hadn't risen, and now only a trickle of weak sunrise crept over the horizon. Neddy knew Sun was nearing its last days. Her stomach turned at the thought of the world falling to Dark. She was hungry and thirsty, and her body ached. She didn't know how much farther she had to go, what else she was going to have to do, but she pushed away the feelings of despair that kept trying to crawl into her head, and forced herself to believe she could do it. She *could*. She *would*. The world would *not* end because her Quest *would* be completed. She would save Sun and Moon and she would do it all before the stars lined up for the Ascension.

She told herself all of that. Again and again. And, this morning, she almost believed it. She was surrounded by friends who believed in her, she knew that. But did she believe in herself?

A wet nose on the back of her neck brought Neddy's mind back to the present. She smiled and wrapped an arm around Dog's neck.

"You're still not sure what that was last night?" Dog asked. He'd asked the night before, several times, before falling asleep.

"No. I'm just glad it showed up when it did," Neddy answered. She didn't know what would have happened if the shadow, or creature, or whatever it was, hadn't chased off the Gloks.

"You know that's not the end of them," said Spider. "The Gloks, I mean."

"Which is another reason we need to keep moving." Neddy watched the churning river falling over the edge of the cliff.

"I could fly down and meet you at the bottom," Crow offered.

"That's very nice of you," said Neddy with more than a hint of sarcasm, "but how does that help *us*?"

"Quaaaw – " Crow started to say something, but turned his head backwards to preen his tail-feathers instead.

Dog carefully tiptoed as close to the edge of the waterfall as he dared. "That's a lot of water going a long way down."

"And it's a sharp drop," said Neddy, "I can't see if there's any way to climb around it." She pulled out the pouch with biscuits, gave a few to Dog, and took one for herself.

Exhausted. Frustrated. With no idea how to do what next. Neddy sat, staring blankly at the nothingness in the unfocused air in front of her, her mind filled with useless thoughts, none of which were capable of forming a single coherent solution, mostly because she didn't know what the question was anymore.

A breeze sifted by, playing with the frazzled wisps of Neddy's hair. It felt cool and it tickled her neck, nudging something inside her. Neddy's eyes cleared and meandered into focus, and she realized it had been a long time since she'd noticed everything around her. She'd been so focused on the hardships, she'd forgotten to feel the air; to listen and hear roots stretching towards moisture; to see, even in the muted light, the little creatures crawling in the dirt. She let her eyes close, let herself smell the aroma of the world, let her mind clear itself of the frustration that had been taking over. And, seeping from her memory to the forefront of her mind came the words... *I am Galenor Nedrick of the Galenorae.*

The breeze picked up, tousling her red curls and tugging at the white stick thrust between the locks. Her hand felt for the twig.

"Why don't I build a boat." It was a statement, not a question.

Dog, who had been resting next to the girl, raised his head and wuffed, "Funny."

Neddy ignored the dog. She stood up, pulled the twig from her hair and held it in front of her. "Why don't I build a boat."

Crow stopped pecking for bugs in the grass and looked up at Neddy. "Quaw?"

"What will you build a boat from?" asked Spider.

Neddy wasn't hearing the others. She was pacing up and down the short length of grass. "I can build a boat." She paced some more. She groaned, "How do I do that? I can't remember!"

"What's she talking about?" Spider looked toward the dog who was now up on four feet, ears perked, tail wagging.

"Back in the cavern," answered Dog, "Karboney said something about her remembering how to build a boat. I didn't know what he meant, though."

"It's the stick." Crow hopped up on Dog's back. "The twig that tries to hold her hair in place."

Neddy held the white twig in both hands. She rolled it between her palms, back and forth, until it felt warm.

"I need a boat," she said, and dropped the twig to the ground.

Everyone watched as the twig did nothing.

She picked it up and dropped it again, this time asking, "Will you please be a boat?"

Everyone watched as the twig again did nothing.

"Quaaw – maybe you should – "

"Hush," said Spider. "Let her think."

Neddy tried asking, tried commanding, tried begging. She tried dropping, throwing, tossing, and sticking the twig in the dirt. Frustrated, she held the thing in the palm of her hand and mumbled words she didn't understand under her breath. The twig shook. Just a little bit.

Ah! That's something, Neddy thought, *I must be getting close.* Gripping the stick in her fist, she whispered to it. "Please be a boat." She closed her eyes, pulled her hands close to her lips, and spoke words she didn't recognize but somehow knew the meaning.

The twig began to vibrate and to tremble. It jumped from Neddy's fist and landed on the grass where it wobbled and shook and bounced once, twice, up high the third time, and came back to the ground as a bigger twig.

Dog wagged his tail some more and tried to encourage the girl. "You're gettin' somewhere."

Picking up the now larger twig, Neddy held it in her hand. Again, holding it close to her lips, she whispered, "Please. I need a boat."

The twig jumped to the ground, bounced around, jumped up high and came back down as a log. Neddy dropped to her knees and slung her body over the piece of wood lying on the grass.

"I can't do it! I've forgotten." Tears formed in her eyes and splashed onto the wood. "What do I do now?" she cried.

Dog wanted to go to the girl, but Spider shook her head.

Neddy draped herself across the white log. She was tired. Tired from walking day after day. Tired from being chased. Tired of things being so difficult. Rebane had never told her how hard the Quest would be. But then, this Quest was different, wasn't it? He couldn't have known, could he? She missed the golem and his lessons. She missed the Galenwood. She even missed the Woman and the Crone. She tried to picture them in her mind and wondered, *Will I ever see them again?*

And, somehow, she heard their familiar voices, saying, "Yes… Yes you will."

Slowly, like a mist rising from the soil, the Galenwood rose in her mind's eye. She saw the trees and flowers. The deer and rabbits running across the field. The lakes and ponds full of frogs. A breeze picked up, moving the leaves and the grasses danced and waved back and forth, their green blades rubbing against each other, creating a susurration that sounded like a hummed song. The song was familiar and Neddy began to hum along with it. The song grew louder and the humming turned to words, and Neddy sang along with the grasses and leaves. It was an old song, in a language from when Mountain and Water first created the world.

A breeze ruffled Crow's feathers. Dog *wuffed* and Spider felt the air. The grass under their feet rustled and began to sway in rhythm with the song Neddy was quietly singing.

And then she remembered.

Neddy wrapped her arms around the log, whispered to it, and stepped back.

Weightlessly, the log rose in the air and hovered for a moment. Then – *foosh*! – it sucked into itself, back into a twig, then a tree, then a log, then, with a loud *crack*! it shattered into hundreds of pieces that spun and swirled and danced their way to the edge of the river. With smacking and slapping sounds, each little piece of wood attached itself to another and another.

First forming a bow then a hull and sides and rounding to a stern. Clicking and clacking. Smacking and slapping. Dust swirling, but not a single splinter. And when it was done there was a white canoe waiting for them on the river's shore.

Without hesitation, Dog ran and jumped into the boat. Neddy followed, gently setting Spider's burlap bag on her lap when she sat down. They looked to Crow.

"I think I'll meet you at the bottom," the bird said and, without waiting for a reply, spread its black wings and flew off in the direction of the waterfall.

Dog watched the bird go and turned to Neddy. "Ummm… how are we going to keep from falling out when we go over?"

"I can take care of that," said Spider, and she jumped to one side of the canoe and then back across to the other, trailing a string of silk behind her.

"Hold on a minute…" Dog watched the spider. "What're you doing?"

"It'll be fine. Just crouch down on the bottom." Spider jumped back and forth across the boat over the girl and the dog, cocooning them between boat and sticky web. "And just in case we get knocked around a bit…" said Spider, as she padded the inside of the hull with the strong silk.

"I'm not so sure about this," Dog wuffed to the girl.

Neddy felt the same but, more than that, she wondered how they were going to leave the shore now that they were securely inside the sticky wrapping. She didn't wonder for long.

When the spider was satisfied enough webbing had been spun, the passengers were secure and the canoe wouldn't take water and sink, she jumped out and hopped to where the boat met the grass. Forelegs against the bow, she pushed with her strong hind legs until the vessel moved far enough into the river for the current to catch it. Then she leaped back into the canoe and burrowed into the webbing.

"This is going to be fun!" she shouted as they rushed faster and faster, bouncing up and down on the chopping waves, towards the crest of the waterfall.

End over end. Side around side. The canoe careened through the water surging down, down, down. It was like being airborne and underwater at the same time. Sometimes they could see glimpses of the sheer cliff alongside the water. It was smooth rock all the way down, as if worked by a stone-smith to remove any protrusion or crag. Sometimes they saw the gray sky that should have been bright blue at this time of day. Mostly it was just water everywhere, washing all around them. Fish fell with them, catching the water with their tails and fins long enough to blink curiously at the canoe and its occupants. Water splashed against the webbing that wrapped the boat, knocking everyone back and forth and, although it was a bit uncomfortable, Neddy felt secure and was grateful how the cocoon cushioned their fall and held the water away.

Pushed by the torrent of water, the canoe dove nose first into the base of the fall. At first, the current held them at the beneath the surface, bashing and rolling the boat like a toy against the bottom of the lake. They broke free, shooting away from the crush and bobbing to the surface. Once the rocking stopped, Spider skipped along one side of the boat and then the other, nibbling at the webbing where it attached to the wood. Carefully, she rolled the bundle of silk into a loose ball, starting at the bow and going toward the hull, picking up the padding on the inside as she went.

It was like having the lid peeled back and, as soon as it was clear, the girl and the dog sat up and looked around. They were in the middle of the lake, small ripples on either side of the boat on the otherwise smooth surface. Gently, a current from the waterfall pushed them across the water, towards the foot of the mountains in the distance ahead.

"Sshhh-t'puk…"

Neddy looked over the edge of the boat, sure she had heard something.

"Sshhh-t'puk."

"Oh," said Neddy, recognizing the voice. "Hello."

"Sshhhnice to see you again," said the water.

"You remember me?" asked the girl.

"Sshhsome of us do," answered the water. "But when you're in a lake, everyone knowsshh as everyone else doesshh…"

A giggle came from somewhere else in the water. "We weren't sshhhure whether you'd get thissshh far."

"I've had some help," Neddy smiled at her friends on the boat with her.

"Friendsshhh are always good," said another part of the water, "and a proper boat helpsshhh too."

Neddy laughed at this. She hadn't laughed in a while.

"Can you hold that open for me?" Spider interrupted, pointing at the burlap bag grasped in Neddy's hand.

"Excuse me," Neddy said to the water, as she turned her attention to helping the spider, pulling the mouth of the sack open so Spider could shove the bale of webbing into it.

"You save that?" asked Dog, cocking his head sideways.

"You have no idea how much work it is to make this stuff." Spider exited the bag after tucking the bundle deep inside it. "It's not something you want to waste if you can help it." She hopped up and onto Neddy's shoulder where she could get a better view of their surroundings.

A shadow hovered over them. Crow circled a few times before landing on the edge of the boat, upsetting the balance. Dog braced his four legs and Neddy reached for either side of the canoe and held on until the rocking stopped.

"That was fun to watch," said Crow. "Quaw. For a bit there I thought you might stay at the bottom of the lake."

Neddy, Dog and Spider each had words for Crow, but they didn't say them aloud.

"It looks like we're being pushed to where we need to go," Neddy said as the canoe began to move. "Thank you," she added, leaning over the side of the canoe.

"Sshhyou're welcome, sshhh-t'puk! You should resshht. We'll bring you acrosshh the lake."

"I'm not a water bird. I'll meet you at the shore." Crow flapped his wings and with a jump flew into the air, making the boat rock back and forth again.

When the canoe had resettled, Neddy and Dog did their best to get comfortable, lying on the bottom of the boat, the girl using the dog for a pillow. Spider climbed back into the burlap sack. Dog began to snore almost instantly. Neddy didn't think she'd be able to, but it didn't take long before the gentle rocking of the boat helped her to fall asleep as well.

Neddy hoped she would dream, but none came to her.

Chapter Thirteen: The Cave

"Quaw. You finally made it," Crow announced, waking Dog and Neddy. The bird was perched on a crag of rock at the base of the mountain where it nudged against the lake. A small patch of clean beach sand bordered between the rock and the water.

"Is there any chance that you could be a little less annoying?" Dog grumbled.

"Not a chance." Crow hopped off his perch and walked across the sand to the boat. "Too much fun."

Neddy climbed out of the canoe. "Did it take us long to get here?"

Dog jumped out of the boat, making sure to kick up some sand in the bird's face.

"Seemed like *forever*," Crow squawked, using his feathers to block the dog's assault.

"Never mind him. It was long enough for everyone to get some rest," said Spider, hopping onto Neddy's arm as the girl slung the bag over her shoulder.

When the canoe was ashore and empty, it rose from the water, spinning and folding into itself, turning back into the white twig and dropping to the ground. Neddy picked it up and stuck it in her hair. She looked along the stretch of beach.

"Okay," said Neddy, "looks like we go this way."

On a nicer day, a day when Sun had all its strength, the beach would have sparkled with crystals reflecting the light. It would have soaked the sun's warmth and the cool of the water. But today it was gray like the sky, and cold. It led them along the side of the mountain for a while, then turned and ducked into a cave. It brought the water with it, holding on with its submerged sand on one side, grasping the foot of the mountain on the other.

Deep they went into the cave. It should have been dark, but there was a faint light filling the cavern. A soft blue glow with a cool white shimmer about it.

"What is that?" asked Dog.

"I don't know," said Neddy. She squinted her eyes, trying to peer into the distance. "It reminds me of the orb."

"Much bigger though," said the dog, "and bluer."

They walked and they walked, the light never seeming to come closer. Now and then Dog would stop to lap up a drink from the lake water. Crow was riding on the dog's back again, only being allowed to do so after promising to keep quiet. A promise neither the dog expected to be held nor the bird intended to keep. But, for now, the crow kept his thoughts to himself and passed the time pecking at tiny bugs and twigs in Dog's coat.

"I don't think we're getting anywhere," Crow said with a mouth full of bugs.

"We *have* to be," said Dog. "You can't walk and not get anywhere."

"I'm just saying… quaaaww… it's all the same." Beady black eyes looked up and around them. "The rocks haven't changed since we got here. See that?" Crow pointed a wing-feather at the side of the mountain where a particularly odd-shaped stone jutted out. "It's been right there the whole time."

They kept walking, with all eyes on the jutting stone.

"Crow's right," said Neddy. She stopped walking. "Something's wrong."

"Quaaaw. Obviously."

Dog shook his back to quiet the bird.

"There's something I'm not seeing..." Neddy murmured to herself. "Something...." She knelt to the ground and leaned her head sideways against the sand, then stood up and waved her arms in the air, around her, above her, in front and in back of her, down to her feet, feeling for something she couldn't see. When all she found was nothing, she stopped and put her hands on her hips.

"Wait," said Spider. "Do that again."

"What?" Neddy said to the spider on her shoulder. "Do what again?"

"Wave your arms around. Like you were just doing."

Neddy waved her arms again. Up. Down. Back. Sideways. Forward.

"There!" Spider gave a little hop, not quite falling off the girl's shoulder. "Right there."

"What? Where?"

"When you wave your hand in front of you. Can't you see it?"

"What's she talking about?" asked Crow.

"I don't see anything." Dog sniffed the air, just in case it might help but it didn't.

"It's like a shimmer," said Spider. "When you put your hand in front of you. Like you're putting it through a curtain."

Neddy waved her hands in front of her again, still seeing nothing.

"Maybe it's because Spider's got more eyes than us," Crow suggested.

"Could be," said Spider. "All I can say for sure is that there is something there."

Neddy took a step back and gathered her thoughts. *Rebane,* she thought, *help me on this.* She closed her eyes and she listened. She could hear the water lapping the sand and the crunch of the beach under their feet. The mountain dropping miniscule pieces of rock, adding to the beach, replacing what the water took away. Bending her knees into a squat, she reached down, scooped a handful of sand and tossed it in front of her. It sifted through the air, stopping mid-air when it hit some sort of barrier, and fell to the ground.

Neddy knelt and flattened her hands on the sand, palms down wriggled her fingers like caterpillars.

Nothing.

Sitting up, she straightened her back, took a deep breath, wiped the grit from her hands, then bent and put her hands to the sand again. Eyes closed. Concentrating.

"There," she said in a hushed voice. "There you are…"

With both hands, she cupped something in her palms and lifted.

"Ayip!" Dog stepped back when the curtain, now being compressed upon itself, shimmered and took solid form.

"It's all the way across the beach," said Crow.

"Told you something was there." Spider didn't want to sound smug but she couldn't help herself.

"Come on, you guys," Neddy stood, holding the curtain up. "Scoot underneath to the other side. I can't hold it forever."

Dog and Crow scrambled under and through.

Neddy dipped under, turning her arms as she went, and let go once she was through.

On the other side of the curtain the light was stronger. It came from what looked like a pond resting in the middle of the beach. It was several paces across – a width that Dog might have been able to jump over with a running start. A blue glow rose from its surface, and a cool white mist formed a dome around it.

Crow jumped off Dog's back and onto the ground. He took a couple of hops to get closer to the glowing dome, and reached out taloned foot to touch it. "It feels soft, like underfeathers."

Not sure where it was coming from, Neddy felt something telling her she needed to step into the pond. Something, or maybe someone, was beckoning her.

"I think I need to do this next part by myself," she said.

"Why?" Dog protested. "We should be there to help you."

"And I want to see what's in there," said Crow.

"I don't know why. I just know I'm supposed to go in there, and I have to do it alone."

"Well," the dog growled just a little, "I don't like it."

"I think… No, I *know* it's going to be fine," Neddy assured Dog. She felt a little bit nervous, not out of fear but of wonder.

She took the burlap bag from her shoulder and set it on the sand, stretching out her arm for Spider to hop down. Reaching into a pocket, she pulled out the pouch of biscuits, opened it, and set it on the ground near Dog. Her hand felt for the pocket where the burlap bag with the heart and breath nestled in it was safely kept, but she didn't take it out.

"I'll be back soon," she said. She shook her arms and let them hang loose at her sides and, closing her eyes, walked through the misty white light and into the dome.

171

~~~~~

Dog wuffed, "Where'd she go? I don't see her anymore." He sniffed the ground where Neddy's footprints faded into the glow.

"She said she'd be okay." Crow hopped anxiously in circles then up onto the dog's back. "She'll be back. Quaw?"

"Be patient," said Spider, sitting back on her haunches. "We just have to be patient."

Dog sat, then lay down, resting his head on outstretched legs, and let out a whimpering sigh. He kept his eyes on the place where Neddy's footprints disappeared.

~~~~~~

Neddy heard Dog's *wuff* and turned to see Spider on the burlap bag, Dog lying on the ground, and Crow perched on Dog's back. She waved to them, not knowing they couldn't see her.

She stepped closer to the pond, watching the blue glow rising from its surface, and realized it wasn't a pond of water. It was a pond of light. At first she thought it to be a pool of borrowed essence from the stars and sun and moon. It was some sort of illumination, but not light. At least, not as she had ever seen light to be.

The air inside the dome felt hazy. And, just as the pond was something she couldn't quite recognize, there was something was in the air, as well. An ether of age and wisdom. Neddy felt ancient time all around her, along with everything that had happened between the very beginning of *then* and *now*.

The distillation of light and air washed over her, pulsating like a beating heart, waves of sighs and breaths. *Water and Mountain*, she thought. Water and Mountain from ancient times. Water and Mountain from the stories Rebane had told her. Water and Mountain that created the world, and the Galenorae. Created her.

A slight ripple moved across the light and a voice floated over the water.

"You are Galenor Nedrick of the Galenorae. You are Neddy."

Neddy heard it without hearing it, like an unspoken whisper into her mind.

"Yes."

"You are here to help Moon and Sun."

Neddy felt incredibly small. "Yes."

"You have found the Moon's breath and Sun's heart."

"I have the breath of the Water and the heart of the Mountain," she reached into a pocket and pulled out the second burlap bag.

There was another ripple, as light and air intertwined, rising together.

"Let us see."

Neddy started to take the items from the bag, then paused. *I can't just set them on the sand,* she thought. She pulled a few red strands from her hair. Rolling them together in her palms, she spoke to them then pulled her hands apart and watched as they wove and knitted themselves together into a small blanket that hovered for a moment, flattened, and gently dropped to lie on the sand in front of her.

Now, carefully, she took the breath and the heart from the bag.

The conch shell was softly white and spiked on the outside, an iridescent rainbow on the inside. From deep within the skeletal spiral, was the roar of rushing waves heaving, splashing, breathing from the lungs of an ocean.

The solid chunk of magma glistened like hot liquid stone. It was warm, and it beat with the pulse of the center of the earth.

Neddy set them both on the blanket.

A sensation of relief washed over Neddy's entire being. She was done. She'd found the breath and the heart. She'd presented them to Water and Mountain. The Quest was complete. She could go home now, in time for the Ascension. *Maybe I have time to visit Karboney and maybe the old woman in the village on my way home,* she thought.

"We were afraid we'd never see these again." The voice was ancient, and soft like a gentle rain, with ages of wisdom in every drop. "We knew we could trust the Galenorae."

I wonder what it will be like... the Ascension... and Neddy imagined what might happen when she returned to the Galen Tower. Her attention snapped back to the present when the voice filled her mind again.

"But you aren't finished," it said.

"What?"

"You need to take the breath and heart to Moon and Sun. If you don't, all will be lost."

Instantly feeling betrayed, Neddy protested. "I can't! How? The Quest – "

"You are to return the breath and heart to Moon and Sun."

"But – " feeling betrayed, Neddy searched for words. "I thought this would be the last thing. My Quest is supposed to be finished."

"This is what must be done."

Neddy stared at the puddle. "Why me?" she asked. "Why did it have to be me who must save the world? I don't know anything. Why couldn't it have been Erda or Gerte? They know so much more than I do."

"Because you are the Girl. Your mind is open. The others *know*. You are willing to *learn*."

"But I don't know what to do." Her voice was small and barely heard. She fell to her knees, collapsing into herself. "I don't know what to do. How...?"

She lay there like that, crumpled and worn out. She'd felt confident after building the boat and riding over the waterfall. Assured when she entered the dome. Relieved when she presented the heart and breath. Now, she felt like a failure. The task was too great. There was no possible way that she could bring the heart and breath to Sun and Moon. She simply didn't know how she could do it. *And so now,* she thought, *all of this for nothing. The world will be in the hands of Dark.*

A soft sigh wisped around her, and another voice spoke. This one stronger.

"Get up."

Neddy didn't want to, but something inside forced her to sit up.

"You *can* do this." The image of Gerte lingered in her mind like thick smoke,

"How am I supposed to bring these to Moon and Sun?," Neddy gestured at the shell and rock resting on the red blanket. "How do I know where to go?"

"They are beneath their horizons." Erda's image joined Gerte's. "Sun has set, and Moon hasn't risen."

Dread churning in her stomach, Neddy thought how the days had grown so dim, and Moon had been barely a sliver the last time she saw it. She knew she had to do something. But *what* and *how* were beyond her ability to imagine.

"That would mean they're on opposite ends of the world," Neddy said. "How can I travel that far?"

"That is something *you* need to find out," said Erda. "And you must do it before the stars align."

"When will that be?"

"Most of them have arrived already, and the others will be here soon."

"But... How?" Neddy felt beaten. Drained of all hope. "How do I help Moon and Sun before all of that happens?"

"Go to the Gloky Mountain."

"The Gloky Mountain?" said Neddy.

"You are very close."

Neddy could feel the air change as the mist sifted back into the pond.

"Wait!" she called out. "Who helped and chased away the Gloks by the river?"

"That was you," Erda whispered. "You have more strength, more power than you realize."

"Wait, you can't go. I need help."

The mist was gone, but Gerte's voice drifted back to the girl, "Find your hero."

~~~~~~

Dog ran to Neddy when she stepped out from the dome. "Are you alright?" He asked, hopping around the girl, sniffing her legs and dress. "We were worried."

"Dog was worried," Crow lied. "I knew everything was going to be alright."

"I'm fine." Neddy smiled, but it didn't match what she was feeling inside.

"So," Spider stood on all eight legs, "what's next?"

"I have to go to the Gloky mountain."

"You mean *we have to go*," said Dog.

"I'd like it if you all came with me," Neddy admitted, "but –
"

"Of course I'm coming with you," Crow said. "You owe me a nest."

"What's a Gloky mountain?" asked Spider.

Neddy realized she hadn't told them what Karboney had told her. "That mound we've been watching grow on the horizon." Neddy waved her arm, pointing in a roundabout general direction. "The Gloks have been building it."

"Building it?" Crow cocked his head. "Out of what?"

"I'll bet I can guess," Dog said, sniffing the air.

"Quaaaaww. that's disgusting…"

"It's just that – " Neddy started.

"It's just that what?" Spider asked gently.

The girl looked at her three friends, feeling as if she would burst from what was swelling up deep inside. She tried to hold on, but couldn't stop it from rushing out. "I don't know if I can do it. I don't know how to get there. I don't know what to do when I get there. I'm supposed to bring the breath and heart to Moon and Sun. But they're not traveling anymore. So how am I supposed to do that when they're beneath the world? And I have to do all of it before the stars get here. And they're already lining up. Most of them are here already. The others will join them soon. And if I don't get these to Moon and Sun in time Dark is going to take over and nothing will matter anymore and all of this," she gestured wildly at everything, " will be for nothing!" She plopped herself on the sand, putting her head in her hands.

Everyone stood in silence.

"Well," Crow gurgled after a moment, "that was a lot."

"You know that we'll help you," Dog said softly, nudging at Neddy's shoulder.

"I know....," Neddy put a hand on the dog's head and scratched behind his floppy ear.

"One thing is certain," Spider said. "We can't do any of it if we stay here."

"But where do we go?" Neddy asked. "I don't know where to begin."

"We're under the mountain now… right?" Dog asked.

"Yeah, I guess so."

"They're probably under it," the dog said, "like they were under the tree."

"You smell it, too?" Spider said to the dog.

"Yeah…" Dog sniffed the air. "It's coming from that way," the dog said, nodding his head upward and to the side. "I'll never forget that smell."

Chapter Fourteen: The Gloky Mountain

They stood at the end of the tunnel, looking down into the pit of filth and stench where the Gloks burbled in the muck, plodding in circles and climbing up the side of the mountain.

"Quaaawww…. what are they doing?"

"Shhh…" Neddy hushed the bird

Spider, holding onto Neddy's shoulder, leaned forward as far as she dared. "It looks like they're swimming around, trying to get as much of that stuff on them as they can."

"Can I have another one of those mint-stones?" Dog asked.

Neddy reached into her pocket and took out a handful of pebbles. They were small and round, each with a tiny rune etched into its surface and softened with whispers so they'd melt in the mouth. She'd made them earlier, when they were nearing the pit and the stench was becoming unbearable. Neddy gave one to Dog, a very tiny one to Spider, and she took one for herself. The minty vapor filled her senses as she sucked on the stone, blocking out the smell of Glok.

Crow cocked his head sideways. "Can I have one of those?"

"You don't need one," Neddy answered. "You don't have a sense of smell, and I don't want to run out before we're done."

"Aw, c'mon," Crow wheedled. "Just one. I want to know what they taste like."

"If it'll shut the bird up," Dog said, "you can give him one of mine."

"Are you sure?"

"Yes," the dog grumbled, "the stench is the lesser of the two."

"Thank you," the bird squawked.

"Shhh!" Neddy said again, and gave a small pebble to the bird. Then she turned back to the pit. "Why would they be trying to scoop it up all over themselves?"

Spider pointed to the trail of Gloks climbing the side of the mountain. "We can probably find out if we follow them."

"How are we going to do that?" asked Dog.

"Quaw. Easy. You just fly on up there."

Dog had lost all patience with the bird some time ago, and answered Crow with a growl. Crow pulled his feathers tight to his body and squatted to the ground.

"Dog's right," Neddy said, "it's a sheer cliff. The only way the Gloks can do it is because they're sticky with that muck."

"I have an idea," said Spider, and she scurried into her burlap bag. A moment later she was pushing a bundle of websilk from the sack. "I knew I saved this for a reason."

~~~~~

"Come on, Crow," Spider called over her shoulders, "put your beak into it!"

The bird and the spider stood on a chunk of rock that jutted from the mountain, pulling on the thin line of silk. At the other end of the line was Neddy, hanging on with her feet and hands, and Dog, swinging in a webbed hammock.

"In any other circumstances," the dog groused, "this might be fun."

Crow grabbed the line in his beak and stepped backward, digging his toes into the stony crag. Spider, in front of the bird, leaned back on her haunches and pulled the silk hand over hand over hand over hand.

"Just hold on. We're almost there," said Neddy, although, with her eyes scrunched as tight as they were, she had no idea how much farther it was to the top.

"Only a few more pulls to go," Spider called down.

Crow tried to say something, but changed his mind when he opened his mouth and the silk line slipped.

"Whoa!" Neddy called out when the rope dropped then jerked to a stop. "What was that?"

Dog was swinging like a pendulum.

"That was the bird," Spider answered, giving Crow a scolding look. "Hang on. We've almost got you."

The spider was right and, with a few more yanks and grunts and pulls, the girl and the dog were sitting on the jutting rock.

"How many is that?" Crow asked, flopping onto his back, feet straight up in the air, panting.

"Three, I think," said Spider. "It's probably better not to count."

Neddy looked down, and then up. The distance was the same in either direction.

~~~~~~

They weren't sure how long it had taken to reach the top of the mountain. It wasn't the tallest, but it was the closest to the Gloky.

"That webbing cut grooves in my beak," Crow complained, running a feather along to its point. "There's ridges!"

Dog lay on his belly, all four legs stretched out to his sides, grateful for the solid ground. "I think I might be sick."

"Oh, stop complaining," Spider admonished them both.

"Spider's right." Neddy said, "There's no time for that. We might be at the top of this mountain, but we're not done yet."

The girl and the spider turned from their companions and looked at the Gloky Mountain stretching to the dark sky. On every side of the mountain, Gloks were climbing up and stacking themselves, one on top of the other. Sometimes a Glok would slip in its own offal and fall, taking the ones below it, as it splattered down. But they never gave up. And the mountain grew and grew, until it was taller than the tallest mountain in the range.

"Why do you think they're doing that?"

"I don't know," Neddy answered. She looked up, then down, then up again. "Oh, no!" she gasped. "They couldn't be – "

"What is it?"

Neddy pointed to the sky, to the string of stars crossing the expanse from one horizon to the other.

"Do you see those stars?" Neddy groaned. "The bridge is almost complete."

"Stars?" asked Spider. "Bridge?"

"When it's time for the Ascension, the stars will form a bridge between Moon and Sun. It's how they combine their power."

"What does that mean?" asked Spider, not sure if she wanted the answer

Neddy thought for a bit. "I don't know, but if I were a Glok and I tried to steal the breath and the heart, but I lost it, I would try something else."

Neddy looked up again. "I think they're trying to reach the stars so they can stop them from forming the bridge. They have to stop the Ascension so that Dark can take over."

"Quaaawww..." Crow hopped over to stand between the girl and the spider, "you still haven't told us what the Ascension is..."

"No time," Neddy said, sounding more abrupt than she meant to. "I have to get to Moon and Sun. Before it's too late."

"I have an idea," Dog grunted, pulling his legs in beneath his furry body and pushing himself into a sitting position.

"Will it involve me pulling you up by the web again?" Crow squawked.

"No."

"I don't want to do that again."

"That makes two of us."

"Let's hear it," said Spider.

"Climb the Gloky Mountain and jump up to the stars."

Neddy looked at the oozing tower of Gloks. "You want me to climb up that?"

"And when we get to the stars, ask them what they would do," said Dog. "They *are* heroes, right? Shouldn't they be able to help you?"

Neddy looked again at the mountain. "I don't think I have enough mint-stones to do that. I don't think there's enough mint-stones in the world to do that."

"Well," Dog lay down on his belly again, "it was just an idea. Didn't seem like anyone else was coming up with anything."

"You're right." Neddy gulped and looked around at her friends. "I don't think I have any other choice."

"No," said Spider. "*We* should do it,"

"I'm feeling better." Dog rose to his feet. "Let's go."

Neddy steeled herself, checked to secure the twig in her hair, and began to climb.

It was the worst experience she'd ever had in her long, long life. Even going under the Glok tree wasn't as bad as this.

Instead of grabbing onto rocks, she grabbed fistfuls of Glok that oozed between her fingers and down her arms. Her bare feet weren't doing much better, with slugs of Glok wedging between her toes.

Spider rode on Neddy's shoulder, and Dog walked sideways in a sort of zig-zag. Crow flew above, cawing unsolicited instructions down to them.

They were about two-thirds of the way up the disgusting climb when, right in front of Neddy's face, a Glok eye opened and stared at her. Shocked with fright, Neddy froze. The Glok reached out with a dripping arm, grabbed her ankle, and yanked her down.

Losing her grip, Neddy began to tumble down the lumpy side of the mountain. Eyes and mouth shut tight to block the muck, she swallowed the shriek that wanted to escape. She could hear Dog barking. It seemed to be getting farther and farther away, but that could have been because of the glop that was slopping into her ears. She grappled with her hands and feet, but everything she grabbed gave way and she continued to roll over and over, down and down.

Don't panic, she thought. *Think of a way out of this.* She concentrated, forcing her mind to stop thinking of how wrong things were going, and focus on finding a way to make it go right.

Whoosh! A rush of wind swept around her, and her fall came to an abrupt, but very welcome, halt. Something that felt like a soft blanket wrapped around her, and, daring to peek open one eye, she found herself swaddled in a dark gray shadow. Spider, still clinging to her shoulder with all her legs, slowly opened her eight eyes and looked around.

Like a smoky cocoon, the shadow rose with Neddy and Spider inside. Dog's barking grew closer and when they reached him a tendril wrapped around him and pulled him inside.

"Quaw!" Crow squawked when a vaporous coil reached out and pulled him inside with the others.

Neddy closed her eyes. Stomachs lurched as they shot upwards, up and up, not stopping until they were high above the mountain of Gloks.

The cocoon opened and hovered flat, like a rug of smoke.

"That was you, wasn't it?" said Dog.

"Yes," Neddy answered, smiling through the muck on her face. She pulled the skirt of her frock to wipe her face clean, but all it did was move the sludge around. She stopped, looked at her equally sludgy friends, and laughed. She laughed harder than she remembered ever laughing before. So many days of frustration, of fear. So many times trying and trying again, sometimes with success, often with failure. So much trouble and worry. It all bundled itself into a ball in Neddy's chest and, with a burst of laughter, was thrown out of her body and sent to the farthest reaches of the universe.

Dog, Spider and Crow at first looked at her with concern. But Neddy's glee was infectious, and soon they were all laughing until their sides hurt. It was exhilarating.

After catching their breath, Neddy looked at the bridge of stars that was almost complete between the two horizons where Moon and Sun were resting.

"They need Moon and Sun to look over their horizons before the bridge can connect them."

The momentary joy gave way to worry once again. But now there was more determination within the worry, and less despair.

"We need to reach the bridge," said Dog. "Can you make this go up that high?"

Neddy concentrated, whispered, tried with all her might to make the shadowy carpet rise some more. Exhaling all the breath inside her, she shook her head. "I think I used it all up."

"So what do we do?" asked Spider.

"I have an idea," said Crow and, without any further explanation than that, he flapped his wings and flew up towards the bridge.

Neddy, the dog and the spider watched as Crow flew, spiraling as he went higher and higher.

"Eh," said Spider. "Now that's just showing off."

"I can't see him anymore," said Dog. "Can you?"

"The sky's too dark. Black bird. Black sky." Spider sat back on her hind legs, resting on Neddy's shoulder. "Now we just have to wait, I suppose."

"Do you have any whispers that might help?" said Dog.

"I've been whispering this entire time," Neddy answered.

They sat down, on the hovering carpet of mist, and they waited.

They waited for what seemed like a long time to Dog and Spider, and even longer to Neddy. She fought back worries, and instead made promises to the universe. She promised Crow would make it back. She promised it would not be too late. She promised she would be able to reach Moon and Sun, and when she did, they would give them their breath and heart. *It's not too late,* she promised.

"This *will* work," she said. "It's not just for us or for the Galenorae. It's for everyone." And she added, under her breath, "For everything."

The three watched the sky, barely breathing.

And then...

"What was that?" Spider said, standing on all eights.

"What?" Dog wuffed, raising his head off his outstretched legs.

"Look," Spider pointed with a long, hairy leg, "that star."

"What? I don't see any—"

"There!" Neddy jumped up. "I see it. It's... it's moving."

"Ayip!" Dog barked. "More than one."

Above them, a small string of stars was falling from the sky. Linked together, they glided through the darkness, leaving a trail of light as they descended. It wasn't all of the stars, but enough to light the carpet as they neared. The rest of the stars stayed in the sky, anchored to either side of the horizon, where Moon and Sun should have been.

Crow led the way, resting at Neddy's feet when he landed.

"You did it." Neddy said barely above a whisper.

"Of course I did," Crow ruffled his feathers. "Was there any doubt?"

Dog *gruffed* and Spider rolled her eight eyes.

Neddy turned to the heroes floating in a circle overhead. *How do I talk to them?* she thought.

As you are now, a voice purred. *It is nice to meet with you again.*

It was a familiar purr. One that pulled a chord far back in Neddy's mind. A chord she couldn't quite place. *Do I know you?*

We were once very close, it answered.

From somewhere in the back of her memories, Neddy knew. *You were Gerte's teacher.*

Yes.

Neddy fought the urge to ask questions. So many questions.

The bird told us you need help, the voice of another hero bleated in Neddy's mind.

Where are Sun and Moon? a voice croaked *What has happened to them?*

We can smell the Gloks, another yipped. A coyote? A wolf?

It's the Dark, Neddy thought.

"What's going on?" Dog wuffed at the lights hovering over them.

"I think they're talking to each other," Crow said. "They don't talk like we do. It was very strange, up there with them. They put their words into your head."

Dark wants to take over the world, Neddy thought.

Dark has always wanted that, said the purr.

Dark might win if I don't complete my Quest. I've gotten this far, but – Neddy took a deep breath – *but I don't know what to do next.*

Tell us. This time it was the voice of an owl. *What do you need? How can we help?*

Neddy told the stars about the breath of the Water and the heart of the Mountain. How they were stolen, how they were found, what she needed to do with them. She told them about the Gloks and the mountain of sludge they were building to try to reach the Stars. And she told them of her Quest and how she needed to do everything and return to the Galenwood before the Ascension. She tried not to let the fear creep into her thoughts that there might not be an Ascension.

The stars' voices hummed as they blended their thoughts amongst themselves. Neddy couldn't understand what they were saying. She waited, trying to be patient.

We know what to do, said the croak.

We will return to the sky, said the owl. *You will come with us and will complete the bridge for you.*

For me? Neddy asked.

Yes, continued the owl, *one end will take you to Moon, the other to Sun.*

And I will walk your bridge to them, she thought, then said aloud, "I'll walk the bridge to Sun and Moon!"

Dog, Crow and Spider looked at the girl.

"Do you know what she's talking about?" the dog said out the corner of his mouth.

"All I know," said Spider, "is that every time she says *I* she means *we.*"

Chapter Fifteen: The Bridge From Moon to Sun

It was cold, and the higher they went the colder it got. Neddy held on to the star, its core warming her, and she wondered how the crow flew this high without his feathers turning to ice. Dog held onto the star next in line, Crow riding on the dog's back with talons digging into the matted hair. Spider hid deep inside the burlap bag slung over Neddy's shoulder.

We're almost there, the hero's voice purred in Neddy's head and, although didn't remember having met the cat, it felt like they were old friends.

Here we are, the bleating voice said.

Neddy felt a tug as if being swung at the end of a rope, like the whip of a snake's tail, as the string of heroes stretched out, the one on each end grabbing the others that were waiting, strung across from horizon to horizon. She felt the voices, moving in waves in either direction. The collective of thoughts passing along the message of Neddy's story – her Quest, Dark, and the help she needed – humming in her mind, and she could feel it in the vibrations along the line. Wave after wave, pulsing from end to end and back again. Louder. Stronger.

"Wait!" Neddy called out. "The dust! I haven't gotten the dust from the sky."

But the waves continued to grow.

Balancing as best she could, Neddy reached into a pocket and pulled out the wooden box Gerte had given her on the Galen Tower. Her hands shook as her fingers tried to untie the golden and pale white strings.

With a great pulse, a wave rose and plunged, and Neddy nearly fell.

"Lean on me," said Dog, as he pushed his body against Neddy's legs.

"Let me do that," said Spider, and she climbed down Neddy's arm to untie the strings.

Neddy lifted the lid from the box. She wasn't sure what she expected to see inside — a vast universe? a sprinkling of glittery magic? a pillow of moss? — and she was surprised that it was just an empty box made of dark, aged wood. She looked to the sky, wondering how to grab a handful of dust without dropping the box.

"Well," said Crow, "I guess I'd better do my share of this." He stretched out his wings, gathered some dust from the sky, and brushed it into the box.

Hurry! a voice bleated as Neddy closed the lid, let Spider quickly tie the strings, and slipped the box back into a pocket. Then it said, *Here we go!*

In a nearly blinding burst of brilliance, the collective light of all the stars, seared through Neddy and a jolting snap almost knocked her over. She steadied herself, then saw a bridge of light stretching from where Sun was resting to where Moon couldn't rise.

You must hurry! The hero's purr was edged with urgency. *We can't hold this for long before Dark sees and comes to break us apart.*

Go to Moon first, a new voice clucked.

Neddy hadn't heard this voice before, but she was sure she recognized it from Rebane's lessons. It was the voice of an ancient tortoise — the first of all the heroes.

"Gilananna." Neddy's breath caught in her throat.

Give Water's breath to Moon, Gilananna gently continued, *and then you must run to give Mountain's heart to Sun. Once Moon has the breath, and it can fill its lungs, it will rise. And Sun must rise with it. When Sun and Moon rise together we will reach across the sky to hold them together. If this does not happen —*

— there will be no Ascension, Neddy finished the thought, forgetting it was the First Hero she was interrupting.

Neddy looked to where Moon slept. The distance was more than it had ever appeared when she'd stood in the Galenwood, looking from horizon to horizon. She whispered to the sky and the air, and to anything and everything that could spare some strength, and she felt the response in a warmth that surrounded her.

Without a word to her companions, she nodded, and she ran. And they ran with her, unquestioning, forever at her side no matter what.

The warm wave of energy traveled with them — at once carrying, pushing and pulling them — towards the end of the bridge and Moon. Neddy's and Dog's hair stood on-end with static and Crow's feathers crackled. The burlap bag rose in the air, the twine being the only thing keeping it from freeing itself.

Inside, Spider wondered whether it might have been a better idea to cling to Neddy's shoulder than to hide inside the sack.

Across the sky, across the bridge, like running on a bolt of lightning, they drew closer and closer to the distant range of mountains. As they neared, they could see Moon sleeping behind the jagged line. A deep sickness struck the pit of Neddy when she saw how its iridescence was gone, smothered by a dull and pale gray. At first the girl thought she might be too late, but when they reached the end of the bridge there was movement as Moon tried to greet them with a weak smile and kind eyes.

Ahhh.... the voice was labored even without being spoken. *A Galenorae. I had hoped to see you one last time.*

Not one last time, Neddy stepped close, *you will see us still, once you're in the sky again.*

No... no more sky... my breath... is gone...

"What are they saying?" Dog barked, prancing on its still-electrified paws.

It's not gone! I have it for you. Neddy reached down to the skirt of her dress and pulled the conch shell from its pocket. *Listen,* she held it to her ear, then up for Moon to hear. *Your breath is in here.*

Moon shifted, lifting itself just enough to see the shell in the small girl's hand. *You found it...*

I had some help. Neddy gestured to her friends.

Thank you… Moon pushed itself from the ground.

I'll see you again, Neddy thought, trying her best to sound hopeful, *at the Ascension.*

"What's she doing?" Dog yipped. The tingling was almost gone from his toes, but the dog still danced. "What are they saying?"

"Hush…" Spider whispered.

Dog, Crow and Spider watched as Moon rolled itself upright. They watched Neddy hold the shell up high over her head. They heard her whisper as she turned the shell upside down, and shook it.

A gust of wind stronger than all the winds of the world put together fell from the overturned conch.

Moon closed its eyes and inhaled.

Neddy reached forward and grabbed a piece of wind with both arms. She muttered something to the captured gust, then yelled over her shoulder, "Hold on to me as tight as you can!"

Dog held the skirt of Neddy's dress between his teeth and wrapped his legs around her body. Crow tangled his talons into the girl's hair and stretched his wings around her head. Spider stayed inside the burlap bag, but not before slinging a fresh string of websilk, securing it to Neddy's shoulder.

Any worry they might have had about running across the bridge to where Sun lay resting was gone as they rode on the wind, over the bridge of stars, through the dark sky, to the horizon on the opposite end of the world. But, even with the force of their own stream of wind, they could feel themselves being tugged backwards as Moon inhaled more and more. Neddy looked over her shoulder and could see it growing brighter, and rounder. She turned to the gust she held in her arms and called out. In response, the wind whipped itself into a spiral, swirling around Neddy and her friends, and carried them faster.

Sun's horizon grew closer, and Neddy could see it behind the mountains, barely flickering, like a faded flame before the fire dies.

When they were close enough, Neddy let go of the wind and dropped down to where Sun was resting. Dog unwrapped himself from around the girl and let the dress fall from his mouth. It took Crow a moment to disentangle himself from the wild red hair, but eventually the talons were extricated and the bird hopped onto Dog's back. Spider peeked out from the security of the bag, and jumped onto Neddy's shoulder when she saw it was safe.

Hahaha…. Sun rumbled a low laugh, *a Galenorae. Which one are you?*

"I felt that," said Dog, sniffing at the trembling ground.

"Sun's not like Moon," Crow said with newfound reverence.

I'm Galenor Nedrick.

I've heard of you… I've watched you… Like Moon, Sun's voice was labored with effort. *They call you… Neddy…*

Yes, I go by Neddy.

The Gloks stole my heart… and Moon's Breath…

I know. But I got them back!

You?

I had help.

Sun looked around. *I don't… see… the other… Galenorae…* every word was a struggle.

No, not the Galenorae. Dog, Crow and Spider helped me.

The ground shook again as Sun chuckled weakly. *Ahhh…you've found your heroes…*

Neddy hadn't thought of her friends in that way. They were her friends. They stuck with her, as friends do. They helped her, as friends do. Then she thought *Yes, they are my heroes.* And she smiled at the three of them.

"What?" Dog wagged his tail.

I feel the air rushing away from here, Sun adjusted itself to better face the girl. *Moon has the Breath again?*

Yes. We just came from there. And now, Neddy dug into the pocket that had opened just at the right moment, *here is Mountain's heart.*

Sun looked at the pocked stone, cool on the outside, pulsing with molten rock on the inside.

I remember Rebane teaching me that you wear this on your belt, thought Neddy.

Rebane, that old Fox. Yes, that's correct. But...

Neddy wanted to wait for Sun to finish the thought but her impatience got the better of her. *But...? What?*

I am too weak.

Too weak for what?

The heart lives in the clasp of my belt... I am too... weak... to open it.

Neddy looked closer and saw the belt of fire wrapped around Sun's belly. *Maybe I can do it for you.*

The clasp can only be opened with the tiniest spark. Even if it didn't burn you to an ember, it is too small even for your little hands to reach inside and unlatch it.

There must be a way, Neddy thought. *It can't be over. Not now. Not after... everything!* She turned to her friends. "We need to think of something. The heart needs to go inside the clasp, but my hands are too big. I can't do it. And Sun's too weak."

"I'll do it," Dog yipped.

"You're too big, too." Neddy said, "And, besides, I don't think your paws could open the latch."

"Let me try!" Dog whined.

"My beak is sharp," said Crow, "but it's not much smaller than your fingers... or those paws."

"Give it to me," said Spider.

"It's too big," said Neddy. "Too heavy for you."

"I may be small, but I am very strong." Spider looked at the three friends facing her. "I don't mean to brag, but I'm stronger than any of you. Probably all of you combined." She turned towards Neddy. "Give me the Mountain's heart."

Neddy hesitated.

Without warning the bridge they stood on jerked downward. *There's not much time left...*

Neddy heard Sun and looked towards the far horizon where Moon was beginning to rise. And between her and Moon the bridge was sinking and she thought, *Why is it falling?*

It's not falling. Look harder. It is being pulled down.

Neddy looked again, and saw a stretch of putrid muck on the bridge. An arm made of melded Gloks rose, and the hand attached to it grabbed at the bridge, jerking it back and forth, pulling it down towards the Gloky Mountain.

"We have to hurry!" Neddy exclaimed.

"Give me the heart," Spider said with calm assurance. "Let me do this for you."

Neddy handed the red stone to the spider. "Please be careful."

"I will," said Spider. "You wait here. I'll be right back."

Spider hoisted the stone with her forelegs and, walking on her hindlegs, carried it towards Sun.

The bridge jerked again, but Spider kept her balance.

As she neared Sun it wasn't as hot as she'd expected. But then, she remembered, Sun was weak. Trying not to imagine the flames that would most likely erupt when she placed the heart inside the clasp, she looked over her shoulder. Dog was sitting, anxiously panting, his two front feet restlessly stamping. The bird was squatting, as if in an invisible nest, its beady black eyes unblinking, watching her. Neddy stood, holding her hands clasped in front of her. Spider thought she saw the girl whispering, but maybe it was just the flicker of shadows. Either way, she moved ahead.

Spider slipped backwards when the bridge bent downwards. She could feel the stars beneath her tiny claws – so taut she feared they might snap – and she dug her toes in, fighting to stay in place. She needed to do this. Giving her friends a quick smile and a nod of her head, she turned again towards Sun.

The stone in her arms was huge compared to her small body, and it blocked her view. To make her way, she used her pedipalps to sense the air, feeling the shape of the belt and its buckle in the warm waves flowing from the sun. When Spider reached the clasp, she shifted the heart to three of her forearms. She stretched the fourth into the very small opening and, after letting the hairs on her leg feel around, pulled on the tiny latch. The front of the clasp swung open, almost knocking her over. But she held herself in place, and when she had her feet beneath her again, she lifted the stone up and shoved it into the buckle.

That was the last thing Spider remembered.

Chapter Sixteen: The Hero

Neddy looked around. To one side, Dog floated, gently tumbling, a look of wonder on his face. To her other side, Crow was flapping his wings against air that wasn't there. Her own red hair wafted around her face, getting in her mouth and eyes. She brushed it away. All around her it was dazzling white, and a sense of relief washed over her. She closed her eyes, knowing this peace, this serenity, would not last long.

She was right.

A din of *quaws!* and *aiyips!* and a hard *thump!* broke Neddy from her trance, and she rolled across the flat surface of the Galen Tower, tumbling end over end – paws, legs, talons, arms, a beak, hair, and a tail – a tangled ball of dog, bird and Galenor.

A large obsidian hand reached down and stopped them from falling over the edge of the tower.

"You've done it."

Neddy looked up into the golem's black eyes, disoriented. It took a moment for her to realize where she was. And then she jumped up and hugged her teacher. "Rebane!"

Rebane returned the hug, very briefly, then, his hands of stone on her shoulders, turned her around.

Erda and Gerte stood before her. It felt good to see them smile. But the moment was short-lived.

"No time to waste!" said the old woman. "Which one is your hero?"

Neddy's head was still settling into place. She looked at the dog and the bird. Something was missing. When she realized what it was, her hands went to her face and she gasped, "Where's Spider?"

"Is this who you're looking for?" The golem held out his hand, and a tiny spider lay crumpled on the upturned palm.

"Spider!" Crow, Dog and Neddy burst at once, and ran to Rebane.

The golem gently pushed them back. "Not too close," he said, "she's hurt."

"Oh, Spider," said Neddy.

"Did I do it?" Spider asked, her voice weak and barely above a whisper. "Did it work?"

"You did," Neddy cried. "You saved us. You saved us all. You saved the world."

"That's good." Spider took a deep breath and closed her eyes.

"No!" howled the dog.

"Hush," Spider said out the corner of her tiny mouth, "I'm not dead yet. Just... resting...."

"Neddy!," Crone called loudly across the clearing atop the Galen Tower. "You must choose your hero. Now."

"It must be done before the Ascension begins," said Erda, and she pointed up to where all the stars of the sky had formed their bridge from one horizon to the other. "Sun and Moon are at either ends of the world and the stars are holding their bridge between them. But they won't stay like that forever."

"I know." Neddy looked at her friends. "But I don't know. How do I choose?"

"What does a hero do?" Crow asked, once again standing on Dog's back.

"When the Ascension begins, the golem will once again be two. Golem Rebane will return to being Obsidian and Erda's hero, Rebane the fox. My hero – one of you – will join with the obsidian and become the new golem for the new Galenor Girl."

"So," said Crow, "if I'm not the hero I get to watch the Ascension?"

"I guess so…"

"That settles it for me," the bird said, ruffling his feathers.

"Never mind the bird," Dog said, tilting its head towards the spider in Rebane's hand. "We all know who it has to be."

Neddy nodded and went to Spider. "Will you?" she asked.

"Of course I will," Spider answered. She tried to smile, but it hurt too much.

"After the Ascension, each of the Galenorae will transform in a succession to the next stage. Crone will be Girl, and she will remember nothing. She will be innocent, and you will teach her."

"I can do that." Spider closed her eyes, breathed deeply, and slowly opened them again. "Happily."

"We've only known you as Spider," said Neddy. "Do you have a name you might be known by?"

"No… I don't suppose there's ever been a need."

"Well," said Neddy, "we could go with Spider, but that would mean the next golem's name will be Golem Spider…"

"Ah..." said the spider. "I see what you mean." She thought for a moment, then said, "I've always liked the name *Araneae*."

Neddy beamed. "Then it will be Golem Araneae."

"Time's running out!" Crone called out. Neddy nodded, and each of the Galenorae went to their places.

On the flat surface of the Galen Tower were three lines, carved deep, their ends touching so they formed a perfect triangle. Runes were etched into the stone inside the triangle, and at each tip was a sigil.

One sigil represented wisdom, knowledge, and eldership. Crone stood on it.

One sigil represented life, consideration, confidence, and strength. Woman stood on this sigil.

One sigil represented youth, innocence, wonder, and learning. Neddy pulled the dark wooden box from her pocket, handed it to Rebane, and took her place standing on this sigil.

Rebane stood in the center of the triangle, gently setting Araneae down beside his feet. He gestured for Dog and Crow to stand back. A shadow crossed over them, and Arawn, Gerte's lammergeier, floated down on enormous wings. It went to the Crone, nudging the old woman's forehead with its large, curved beak before joining Rebane and Araneae. The three heroes faced each other, forming a circle. Rebane untied the strings from the box with his large fingers, set the box on the ground in the center of the circle, and opened the lid.

The three Galenorae reached out their arms, sparks erupted from their fingertips, crackling in the charged space between them. A stream of energy poured down from the bridge of stars, connecting with strands of white fire. The dust from the sky rose from the box, stretching into ropes, and the mist in the air became twines of water. The fire, water and earthen cords wove and braided themselves, extending along the lines of the triangle and, when the three were bound together, the geometric pattern burst into a beam of light rising high, up to the stars strung across the sky, where it split, sending waves in every direction across the world

As each wave reached its terminus, heroes' voices spoke ancient words. Words older than the world. And those words filled the waves of light, sending them back to the Galen Tower where they merged into a ball. A giant orb of fire, earth, water and air.

The pendants on the Galenorae's ring, bracelet and necklace glowed to fill the orb, swirling with the elements in the dance of every Ascension.

Dog and Crow watched as inside the orb the Galenorae rose, each floating above their sigil. The sigils glowed, then burned, and a whirlwind spun inside the orb, picking up Woman, Crone and Girl, hovering over the Golem.

An explosion of white light filled the orb, nearly bursting the edges of the floating sphere with all the energy of what created everything.

Dog covered his eyes with a paw, and Crow buried his face in Dog's coat, as the brilliance radiated across the surface of the Galen Tower.

Finally, the orb dissipated and the bridge in the sky broke apart as the Stars returned to their distant sky. This time, one more, Arawn, joined them.

In the center of the triangle stood Golem Araneae, black obsidian with streaks of orange and tiny hairs on her arms and legs. She smiled at Dog and Crow. The wooden box rested at the golem's feet, with its lid closed and the golden and pale white strings tied across it. A red fox sat next to the golem's feet. He looked around then went to the Galenor at the Crone's sigil, bringing the box with him.

Erda raised her head and, when she saw the fox, her old friend, her hero, she reached out for him. "Rebane!" she said, holding the animal close.

The fox nuzzled into her white hair. "It suits you," he said, sniffing the ring on the old woman's finger and nuzzling into the cowl-covered black dress. The fox gave the small box to the Crone, and she slipped it into a pocket of her dress that had appeared then disappeared once the box dropped into it.

Neddy sat up, looking at the red leggings and tunic she now wore. She reached for her neck and clutched the fine, braided-silver necklace with a sun-and-moon pendant dangling from it. She ran her hands through the thick black hair cascading down her back, a few wild strands teasing to be free. Then she turned around.

Dog and Crow stood in bewilderment. Dog sniffed the air warily, suppressing a growl. Crow leaned backwards, cocking his head sideways, his beady black eyes darting from one Galenorae to another.

"It's me," said Neddy. "I look different, but I'm still Neddy."

Dog gingerly stepped closer to the woman. But once convinced, he jumped on her and licked her face. Crow watched, waiting for Dog to finish so he could hop back onto the dog's back.

They turned to Spider who was now Golem Araneae.

"How do you feel?" asked Neddy.

"Strange. Odd." The golem moved her arms around. "Fewer legs than I'm used to." She blinked her eyes of stone. "Fewer eyes, too. But," she smiled warmly, "this is delightful."

They stood for a bit, happy to be together. Happy to be done with the Quest. Then Neddy looked to the sigil where she had been standing at the beginning of the Ascension. A girl who looked to be about twelve years of age was sitting there. Berry-red ringlets bounced on her head and her white dress was immaculate. On her small wrist she wore a braided silver bracelet with a pendant that had a sun on one side and a moon on the other.

Neddy took the golem's hand and led her to the girl. "Girl," said Neddy, "I'd like you to meet Golem Araneae."

"Pleased to meet you," said Araneae, reaching out a massive obsidian hand.

"Hello," said the Girl.

"Araneae is going to be your teacher," said Neddy. "Do you have a name you'd like to be called?"

The Girl thought for a moment, then said, "I think I'd like to be called Brighid."

~~~~~~

And so, for the next five hundred years, Golem Araneae taught Brighid, the Girl, everything she needed to know about the world; Erda, the Crone, kept the secrets and knowledge of the world; and Neddy, the Woman, the Goddess of the Galenwood, watched over the world called Galen, with Dog and Crow at her side. They often visited with Golem Araneae, and they looked forward to when she would be Spider again, rejoining them at the next Ascension.

The End

To my reader

Thank you so much for reading *Saving Sun and Moon: The Quest of the Almost-Goddess*, and I hope that Neddy, Dog, Crow and Spider feel like friends for you as much as they do for me.

As an indie-author, I would so, so much appreciate it if you could take a moment to leave a review. That's what keeps us writers alive in these literary ventures.

Saving Sun and Moon began as a short story about a girl who was an apprentice to an old crone-witch, and whose lack of attention to detail caused her to be followed home by some... *mistakes*. After writing it, the idea rolled around in my head until it became this book. It was so fun to write.

I like to include a little bit of my own family's jokes and such in my stories. Gloks is one of them. When I was little, my family would spend time at the beach along the river. We'd play in the mud, picking up handfuls and letting it ooze through our fingers, running and dropping and plopping down into a small mountain. We called these *gloky mountains*. It wasn't until much later that I put 2-and-2 together, and realized my mother called the poop in my little brother's diaper *gloky-glocks*. So, yeah, we were making poop mountains, with our mom laughing as we did it.

If you have questions, comments, or just want to say *"Hello!"* I would love to hear from you. You can email me at sorchamonk@sorchamonk.com or find me on twitter @sorcha_monk and on Facebook as Sorcha Monk, author.

About little bit about me

When I read a story, I like knowing a little bit about the person who wrote it. So, here's a little bit about me...

I was a middle school teacher for almost 20 years, but that was in another life. Nowadays, when I'm not writing, I spend my time playing in the clay with pottery, riding my motorcycle, walking my dogs, and bowing down before my cats.

You can probably tell that I love animals. Growing up, there were always dogs and cats in my family. We had a couple of Mustang horses that we rode bareback, and lizards and tortoises and birds... but mostly dogs and cats.

At the time I am writing this, I live in the town where I grew up. In a desert, near a river with a wildlife refuge, and surrounded by mountains. In one direction, the mountains are desert with giant rocks worn into shapes and caves by years of erosion. In the other direction, the mountains are forest, covered with trees.

For as long as I can remember, I have enjoyed reading. I was the kid who always had a book, and my library reading-punchcard was full of holes. Today, I'm the one with the ebook (because I can't carry all the books I want to read). I have always loved stories – especially the good ones – and I hope that for you, *Saving Sun and Moon: The Quest of the Almost-Goddess* has been a good one.

Upcoming books by Sorcha Monk

The Goblin Chronicles
Book One: The Goblin's Eyes
Book Two: The Goblin's Castle
Book Three: The Goblin's Tea Party
(and more to come)

(There are lots more books, but they're still inside my head.)

SORCHA MONK

Made in the USA
Columbia, SC
12 February 2024

31295050R10138